Emily Harvale lives in Ea
although she would prefer
Alps…or Canada…or any____ ___ __ __ _____
months of snow. Emily loves snow almost as much
as she loves Christmas.

Having worked in the City (London) for several
years, Emily returned to her home town of
Hastings where she spends her days writing. And
wondering if it will snow.

You can contact her via her website, Twitter,
Facebook or Instagram.

There is also a Facebook group where fans can
chat with Emily about her books, her writing day
and life in general. Details are on the 'For You'
page of Emily's website.

Author contacts:
www.emilyharvale.com
www.twitter.com/emilyharvale
www.facebook.com/emilyharvalewriter
www.instagram.com/emilyharvale

Scan the code above to see all Emily's books on
Amazon

Also by this author:

Highland Fling
Lizzie Marshall's Wedding
The Golf Widows' Club
Sailing Solo
Carole Singer's Christmas
Christmas Wishes – Two short stories
A Slippery Slope
The Perfect Christmas Plan – A novella
Be Mine – A novella
***

The Goldebury Bay series:
Book One – Ninety Days of Summer
Book Two – Ninety Steps to Summerhill
Book Three – Ninety Days to Christmas
***

The Hideaway Down series:
Book One – A Christmas Hideaway
Book Two – Catch A Falling Star
Book Three – Walking on Sunshine
Book Four – Dancing in the Rain
***

Hall's Cross series
Deck the Halls
The Starlight Ball
***

Michaelmas Bay series
Christmas Secrets in Snowflake Cove

Blame

it on the

Moonlight

Emily Harvale

ISBN 978-1-909917-29-3

Published by Crescent Gate Publishing

Print edition published worldwide 2018
E-edition published worldwide 2018

Editor Christina Harkness

Cover design by JR, Luke Brabants and Emily Harvale

This book is dedicated to dedicated to my lovely
friend, Rachel Taylor.
So many years. So many memories.
Here's to many more.

Acknowledgements

My grateful thanks go to the following:

Christina Harkness for her patience and care in editing this book.

My webmaster, David Cleworth who does so much more than website stuff.

My cover design team, JR.

Luke Brabants. Luke is a talented artist and can be found at: www.lukebrabants.com

My wonderful friends for their friendship and love. You know I love you all.

All the fabulous members of my Readers' Club. You help and support me in so many ways and I am truly grateful for your ongoing friendship. I wouldn't be where I am today without you.

My Twitter and Facebook friends, and fans of my Facebook author page. It's great to chat with you. You help to keep me (relatively) sane!

Thank you for buying this book.

Blame

it on the

Moonlight

Chapter One

Luna Blake peered through the window and half-expected to see gas lamps illuminating the platforms as her train from Gatwick, trundled into Michaelmas Bay station. Unlike so many larger stations, Michaelmas Bay had clearly not had an overhaul since the year dot. With its olive-green and black pillared walls and its rather grandiose, arched, glass and iron roof, it was like being transported back to the Victorian era. Bijou but not quaint or particularly welcoming, it consisted of two platforms either side of two railway lines and beneath its glass canopy, a small concourse where the tables and chairs of a pocket-sized café, sat empty. The whole place presented a rather forlorn appearance on this cold, blustery morning, with a sky at least fifteen shades of grey. It might have been the last day of February but Spring still seemed a long way off.

The train juddered to a halt and Luna was surprised when Severine, the woman she had been chatting to on and off for the last hour and a half, stood up and asked a man nearby to help her with her luggage. He did so willingly, whilst Severine stepped from the train and waited.

'Oh. I didn't realise you were …' Luna let her voice trail off. Severine wasn't listening; her gaze was fixed in the direction of the concourse.

Why hadn't Severine mentioned that Michaelmas Bay was her stop? It was rather odd, bearing in mind that Luna had told her it was where she was getting off. Come to think of it, Severine hadn't mentioned where she was going or where she was staying. In fact, all she had talked about was New York, and Harvey, her fiancé. She had also said how tired she was and had spent a considerable amount of the journey with her eyes firmly closed.

After assisting Severine with her luggage, the man turned to Luna and offered to help with hers. Luna thanked him, but refused his offer and struggled with her battered suitcases as she stepped inelegantly from the train, which resulted in her adding another tiny dent to one and a couple more scratches to the other. The man shook his head in a rather disparaging fashion and returned to his seat.

Luna took a moment to regain her composure. She was a little disappointed that Severine had walked away without so much as a 'goodbye', 'good luck', or even a friendly smile. Luna thought she would have waited so that they could walk along the platform together.

Had she upset Severine in some way? Was it something she had said? Luna could not think of anything. She could hurry after Severine and ask but there didn't seem much point.

Luna buttoned her coat and pulled on her gloves. From where she stood she could view the station in its entirety and counted a mere seven people on the concourse, although for here, that was no doubt considered a crowd. Her uncle, Mason Riley had told her that Michaelmas Bay was a tiny, seaside town. He had also told her that it was ten times larger – if not more – than the miniscule village of Snowflake Cove in which he now lived. He had emailed her several photos of his village, and the ancient Snowflake Inn – his local pub – looked cosy and inviting. Luna hoped Mason's camera did not lie, because cosy and inviting were the exact opposite of the ambiance of Michaelmas Bay station.

Perhaps it looked prettier in the summer when hanging baskets filled with cascading flowers no doubt hung on the dozen or so, now empty, iron hooks, and dazzling sunlight streamed in through the glass roof. Now it merely looked drab. And somewhat deserted.

Was the rest of Michaelmas Bay like this?

Chapter Two

Severine Starr had no intention of waiting for the woman she had been chatting to. She quickly flipped up the pull-along handles on her two suitcases, re-adjusted the strap of her holdall before swinging it onto her shoulder, and marched along the platform. Scanning the excited faces of the three people waiting eagerly by the barrier and the four on the concourse going about their business, she soon realised, not one of them was there to greet her.

She had not expected her family to lay on a brass band to welcome her – especially considering the last few conversations she had had with them – but she had hoped that at least one of them would have checked her flight and train times and come to meet her. Surely her daughter, Raven, could have made the effort, or her own sister, Evie. But clearly not. Not even her once doting Dad was anywhere to be seen. What a great start this was to her homecoming.

Severine sighed with resignation. Hopefully, there would be a minicab outside that could take her the few miles from Michaelmas Bay to her childhood home, the ancient Snowflake Inn, in the 'chocolate-box' village of Snowflake Cove, but she somehow doubted that. She would have to wait for one to arrive, once she'd found the number of a local cab firm and ordered one. She didn't have a number to hand because, until now, whenever she and Raven had come to visit, one of the family had been there, with a minicab waiting outside. If she had known that no one would bother, she would have booked one from the train. At least the carriage had been warm, if not exactly cosy, but this antiquated station was as cold as Siberia. Not that Severine had been to Siberia so she had no real idea how cold the place was. She'd thought it had been cold in New York, but this – this was enough to freeze her fingers off, if they hadn't been clad in the fake-fur lined gloves her fiancé, Harvey had given her at Christmas.

The woman she had met on the train was going her way. What was her name again? Luna? Hadn't she said that her uncle was meeting her, or something? Severine could grab a lift with her, even though that was the last thing Severine wanted. Making light conversation during the journey was one thing – even though she had pretended to sleep for much of the time. Going into details about her family and her life in Snowflake Cove, and why she hadn't mentioned this was her destination, was another. Luna would hear all the gossip soon enough.

Severine shoved her ticket into the machine – one of the few modern additions to the station – and the barriers parted, allowing her to bundle herself and her luggage on to the concourse. She gasped when a young man pushed open one of the double, Victorian, entrance doors and a gust of bitter wind rushed in with him. She had been here less than five minutes and was already wishing she were somewhere else. Anywhere else. She wished she had stayed in New York, with Harvey, but her family had made it abundantly clear that they were less than pleased with her behaviour, and she knew that delaying her return any longer might well have resulted in her being permanently outcast. Which actually might not be such a bad thing – apart from being separated from her daughter, of course. Not that Severine was flavour of the month with Raven, either. Not since that phone conversation when she had told Raven they would be moving to New York, to which Raven had replied, 'Over my dead body!'

Severine shivered, not merely from the cold, but also from the fact that that could have so easily been the case. When Raven and her friend Roland had fallen into the ice-cold, swirling waters around Snowflake Cove at Christmas, things could have ended so differently. Thankfully, they had both been rescued. By none other than the TV star and ex-SAS hero, Zachary Thorn, who was now, apparently, Severine's sister Evie's boyfriend. How strange life could be. The rescue had been a miracle. It had also been filmed by one of Zachary's TV crew, and shown on TVs across the globe within hours of it happening. Which had created another nightmare for Severine. The accident was the reason Roggero Tazzeone had returned. And that had opened up a whole new can of worms. Why did life have to be so complicated?

Severine shivered again and turned to look behind her. Luna was heading towards her and even from this distance, Severine could see the woman was smiling. Oh, what the hell. She'd ask Luna for a lift. How bad could it be?

'Severine? Severine! Is it really you?'

Severine turned again and eyed the young man who had accompanied the arctic blast and who now stood a mere few feet away from her. He was about the same age as her, or possibly a few years younger; thirty-five or so, at a guess, and he was not at all bad-looking. Nothing compared to Harvey, who even made Ryan Gosling look like an ugly duckling in comparison. Well, maybe not an ugly duckling exactly, but Harvey was *hot*. Really, really *hot*. This man was … was …

'Logan? Logan Dorset? Hell's bells, Logan! You've changed.' The holdall slipped from Severine's shoulder and landed on the tiled concourse with a resounding thud.

Logan grinned, his eyes wide and bright as he looked at her. 'It has been more than fifteen years since you last saw me. I'm not the gangly teenager I used to be. At least I hope I'm not.'

His jovial laugh warmed her skin and memories of summers long ago played before her like advertising banners. Gangly teenager would not have been how she would have described him back in those days. He might not have known it, but she had had a bit of a crush on him. Although that had disappeared in a puff of smoke the moment Roggero Tazzeone had shown a particular interest in her.

Better not to think about the past. She had a bright future before her … if she didn't mess it up.

'Have you come to meet me?'

Severine watched his smile fade.

'No.' He shook his head. 'Sorry. I didn't know you were arriving today. As bizarre as this sounds, I'm here to pick up a consignment of oysters. Len Graves – you probably remember him – works here. He lives in the old stationmaster's house and he gets them delivered here by van, from his son's fishery on the Essex coast. The oyster beds there are famous, so naturally, when he said I could have some at a very good price, I jumped at the chance. He supplies several other local restaurateurs, but we all have to come here to collect them. But I can tell by the expression on your face that you couldn't care less about oysters, Len Graves, his son, or my restaurant.'

'Not at the moment, no. I'm freezing. And shattered. It's been a very long trip. I thought one of the family would have come to pick me up but as usual, no one bothers about me.'

Logan's shoulders slumped. 'You haven't changed a bit, Severine.'

'Thank you.'

He frowned. 'That wasn't a compliment.'

Severine opened her mouth to reply but decided it was better to ignore his remark.

Logan continued: 'I'm glad you've finally decided to come home. Not that it's any of my business. Anyway, if you're going straight to the inn, I suppose I could give you a lift. It's out of my way but it'll only take a few minutes. I think I can squeeze you into my van. As long as you don't mind your cases sitting under trays of shellfish and freshly picked vegetables. They may get a bit … messy.'

Severine tried not to screw up her nose. She was cold and tired and wanted nothing more than to warm herself in front of one of the roaring log fires in Snowflake Inn with a mug of steaming hot coffee in one hand and one of her mum's chocolate doughnuts in the other. Logan's less than enthusiastic offer might not be ideal but it meant she wouldn't have to wait around for a minicab, or beg a lift from Luna and answer questions she would rather not.

'Messy? How messy? They're designer, you know, and they cost an arm and a leg. Not that I paid for them. Harvey bought them for me before we went to New York. Haven't you got a plastic sheet or something you could cover them with?'

Logan tensed momentarily, took a deep breath, and shrugged. 'I may have.' He reached into his coat pocket and handed her a set of keys. 'Here. The van's parked out front. Put your stuff in the back and wait for me. You'll have to move the bags of shopping from the passenger seat. I'll be about five minutes.'

She took the keys, and Logan headed towards a gate to one side of the station.

'Which van?' she called after him.

He threw her a sarcastic look over his shoulder. 'This is Michaelmas Bay, Severine. There won't be more than one or two to choose from. Hit the remote and it'll be the one with the flashing lights.'

She sneered at him, but only once he'd looked away.

'Smart-arse.'

She watched him for a moment. He had filled out. He had been tall, slim and agile in his teens. During the intervening years he had grown taller, broader and more athletic-looking. And possibly even more attractive. Evie hadn't mentioned that. But then Severine hadn't really had that sort of conversation with her sister recently. When was the last time she had? Months? Years? Severine couldn't recall. They seemed to have been drifting apart for a long time. Probably since Severine left to live in London all those years ago. The only time she returned to Snowflake Inn was at

Christmas and for one week in the summer. The distance between them would only get worse – in every way possible – once Severine moved to New York.

Logan stopped, turned briefly as if he could feel Severine watching him. Then without so much as a smile, he began loading crates that were stacked just inside the gate, on to a trolley. An older man was chatting to him but he seemed oblivious as he worked and as Severine watched, she remembered why she had had a crush on him all those years ago.

Chapter Three

Luna smiled at Severine as she passed along the concourse but Severine did not return the smile. Severine was clearly too engrossed in her conversation with the rather sexy-looking hunk who had obviously come to meet her. He looked so pleased to see Severine and yet somehow surprised at the same time.

Luna had no idea what that was about, but for a nano-second, she wished that such a great-looking guy would look at her like that.

'You Luna Blakes?'

Luna averted her gaze from the happy couple to the short, tubby, middle-aged man, who was so busy chewing gum that he couldn't string a complete sentence together. Or perhaps his command of the English language was limited. He was holding an A4-sized piece of paper which looked as if several spiders had trodden in a bowl of ink and scurried across it before scrunching it up and wrapping it in their webs. Perhaps the man was studying to be a doctor. He had clearly mastered the penmanship skills. She grinned and shook her head.

'Ah. Many apologies,' the man said, before moving towards the other few passengers who had got off the train behind her.

She reached out and touched his arm. 'Sorry. I am Luna Blake. I was shaking my head because … Never mind. I'm Luna. My uncle, Mason Riley, sent you to meet me?'

The man raised his brows. 'Luna Blakes? To Bell Cottages, yes?'

'Luna Blake. To Bell Cottage,' she confirmed.

With a nod, the man grabbed one of her two cases from her. 'Come.' He waved her forward with his free hand and she fell into step beside him, the wheels of her luggage clattering over the tiled concourse as they made their way towards the large, Victorian doors.

The man pushed one open with his back and held it in place to let Luna pass but an icy blast hit her in the face and she froze on the spot. It momentarily took her breath away.

'Colds, no?' The man's grin revealed a broken front tooth.

'Freezing.' Luna hurried past and rushed towards the only minicab in sight, parked in front of a minivan.

Her uncle had told her on the phone to be prepared for the bitterly cold weather but she had laughed.

'I've experienced UK winters before, Mason. I can still remember how cold it is but as I survived Norway in December, I'm sure I'll be fine.'

'But we've had a particularly cold spell here since before Christmas. The snow we had in December and January has only just cleared and if anything, the weather's grown colder. Bring lots of layers. And thermals if you have them. I'm sorry I can't meet you at the station. But I'll make sure there's a minicab waiting to bring you here. The doctor says I should be able to walk again in a matter of days. Don't forget what I told you. Warm clothes and lots of them. Safe trip, sweetheart.'

'Thank you, Mason. I'll wrap up warm, don't worry.'

And she had. But not warmly enough, it seemed. It hadn't been this cold in Norway when she had visited a friend for Christmas, and to photograph the Northern Lights. Or perhaps it had. But in Norway a person was prepared for true, arctic conditions. In the UK, it was just supposed to be cold. This was like stepping into a freezer. It hadn't seemed this bitter at Gatwick airport, or at Gatwick station, but then she had been rushing to catch the train after her flight from Spain was delayed, so she hadn't had to wait around on the platform. In fact, she had made it by the skin of her teeth. She had not even had time to find a seat and sit before the train departed.

That was how she had met Severine. By falling on to the lap of an elderly gentleman occupying an aisle seat. After profuse apologies, and running over his feet with the wheels of her cases, she had taken a seat beside him. He had looked her up and down over half-moon spectacles, tutted, got up, and with more tutting and shaking of his head, had moved several seats away.

'That's one way to get two seats to yourself,' Severine had said. 'I usually fake coughing and sneezing. That always works. Welcome to railway hell.'

'Thanks. I'm pleased to be here. Not here on the train. I'm pleased to be in England. I'm relocating from Spain.'

Luna had met Severine's look and both of them had laughed although Luna wasn't sure why. Neither of them had said anything remotely funny.

Chapter Four

Logan cursed his luck as he saw Severine watching him stack the crates of oysters. Of all the trains the damn woman could have arrived on, why had she had to arrive on the one that got here the same time as he had. And why, after all these years, did he still manage to sound like a gibbering idiot when he spoke to her? Why couldn't he have said something cool? Or something clever. Or even something complimentary.

He thumped one crate on top of another and tried to forget she was there. Since returning to stay with his gran and work at Snowflake Inn, he had been dreading the day of Severine's homecoming. She was supposed to have been home for Christmas – but she called to say she was getting married in Las Vegas and would come home at New Year instead. Typical Severine. Then Raven had the accident. Everyone expected

Severine to come back after that. But no. Although she did postpone her wedding.

After that, she called to say the weather was too bad and she couldn't take any chances – now that she was pregnant. Was that the reason? Or did it have more to do with the fact that Roggero Tazzeone was back and Severine's secret was finally out? There was a very strong possibility that a few people would have pitchforks waiting to greet her after that news made the rounds. She was probably sensible to delay her return for another month to let the rancour settle. But then Severine always did what was best for her, didn't she? Regardless of what other people wanted, or needed, or felt.

Logan knew that. He knew how selfish and self-centred she could be. How moody, petulant and sulky she was.

But she was even more stunningly gorgeous now than she had been the last time he had seen her, more than fifteen years ago.

Damn the woman. Just when he had decided that it was about time he grew up and faced the facts. He had to get over Severine Starr once and for all. For Christ's sake, the woman was engaged, she was pregnant, and she was moving to New York. What more had to happen before he accepted that she would never, ever, be his?

And yet she had been watching him just now, hadn't she? He shot a look back towards the concourse, but Severine was no longer there. He told himself it didn't matter – but it did.

'Logan? Are you listening to me, lad?'

Chubby fingers prodded Logan's arm.

'Sorry, Len.' Logan hadn't heard one word. 'What were you saying. I've just had a bit of a surprise and it's thrown me off course somewhat.' He straightened up and stretched his muscles.

Len chuckled good-naturedly. 'Something to do with a woman, I'll bet. I was saying, there are plenty more where these came from, if you're interested. You know where I am, so just let me know.'

Logan smiled, stuck his hand in his pocket, and handed over the agreed amount.

'Thanks Len. I appreciate it. I'll definitely be back for more.'

'Right you are. I'll catch you later then. You carry on with your day-dreaming.' He gave Logan a playful nudge and winked at him before ambling away.

Thinking about Severine was more of a nightmare than a day-dream. The problem was, Logan still had feelings for her. He always had. And he was at very real risk of being as madly in love with her now as he had been all those years ago. That last summer when he'd plucked up the courage to tell her how he felt – but hadn't got the chance. The summer his dad had died. The summer that changed everything.

Chapter Five

Severine stuffed the keys Logan had given her into her coat pocket, retrieved her holdall and tossed it over her shoulder. It seemed heavier. She must be even more exhausted than she had thought. Logan could have offered to help her with her luggage. That would have been the gentlemanly thing to do. But he seemed to be as peeved with her as her family was. Although when he had first seen her, she was sure there had been a spark of excitement in his eyes. Perhaps she had imagined it. Not that it mattered either way. She had no interest in Logan Dorset. No interest at all. Simply memories from long ago. She had Harvey. She was moving to New York. Nothing and no one in either Michaelmas Bay or Snowflake Cove was going to change that. She grabbed the pull-along handles of her cases and marched towards the exit.

Severine would have died from frostbite waiting around for a minicab in this weather and the station wasn't much warmer. She braced herself for the icy wind to slash her face as she pushed open one of the station doors, but the cold still made her gasp. Thank heavens for Logan and his oysters. And he was right; there was only one minivan outside. The only other vehicle in sight was a departing minicab.

Severine pressed the remote, heard the click of the locks, and tugged open the back doors of the minivan, hauling her luggage inside. She spotted a blanket and placed it over her cases, making sure to tuck it in at the sides before dashing to the passenger door. Sighing loudly, she grabbed the bags of shopping and two at a time, transferred them to the back of the van. She didn't look at the contents of the bags as she pushed and shoved them into place and she didn't waste much time doing so. The sooner they were in, the sooner she could clamber into the passenger seat, turn the ignition on and set the heater to max.

Once settled, she closed her eyes and waited, her mind drifting back yet again to the last summer she had seen Logan, when he was nineteen and she had just turned twenty-one. He always came to stay with his gran, Jane Dorset in Snowflake Cove for the summer and winter holidays and Severine wasn't sure when she had first started counting the days until his return. She didn't have a care in the world that summer – other than making sure she kept her sister Evie away from Logan as much as possible. She didn't want the competition. She may have been better-looking than Evie but for some unknown reason, most people seemed to prefer her younger sister to her, and Severine didn't like that at all. Logan, it seemed, was no exception. He was constantly hanging around Evie – although Severine often caught him looking directly at her, but he always looked away and turned his attention back to Evie. He was such a strange teenager. Quiet, reserved, polite and distant with her, but with Evie he would laugh and joke and rough and tumble. Severine tried her best to keep them apart. She also did her best to flirt with him, which seemed to strike terror in his veins. Not the reaction Severine wanted from someone she fancied. She hadn't made a conscious decision to fall for him, and it surprised her when she realised she had. What she wanted, more than anything that summer, was for him to take her in his arms and kiss her.

Until that night on the beach when she had bumped into Roggero Tazzeone, who was not just the father of Evie's best friend, but also a long-time friend of the Starr family. She and Roggero had walked and talked, the sand beneath their feet glistening under a sky filled with diamonds and a moon the size of the sun. The flat, calm sea had turned to liquid silver and made hardly a sound as it lapped the shore. In that near silence, Severine had turned to Roggero and asked him what the hell she had to do to get a man interested in her.

'A man would have to be blind to not be interested in you,' he'd said, and he'd looked at her in a way that made her heart race and her skin tingle.

'Would he?' She couldn't help herself. She smiled coyly.

'Yes, Severine. Yes, he would.'

'But … you're not blind, are you, Roggero?'

'No. *La mia bella ragazza.* I'm far from blind.'

It was odd, but the only time Roggero sounded even slightly Italian, was when he said something in that language. Otherwise, he sounded almost as English as she did. But then he had been born and bred in Michaelmas Bay, like his father before him. The nearest the Tazzeones had got to Italy was the pizzeria the family once owned on the High Street in Michaelmas Bay, their forebears having moved to England centuries before. It was called Bella Italia and had been sold off when Roggero had suddenly announced that making pizza was no longer for him.

'Did … did you just call me a beautiful rag?' Severine had asked.

Roggero laughed. 'Do not look so cross, little one. Ragazza means girl.' He reached out and brushed a strand of hair from her eyes. 'I called you, my beautiful girl.'

'Oh. Oh! I'm not a girl. I'm a woman. And I'm not little, either.' She puffed out her chest as if to prove her point. 'But you think I'm beautiful? You really think that?'

'I do, Severine. I think you're very beautiful.'

She looked deep into his eyes and what she saw heightened her excitement, made her more reckless, more carefree, sexier than she had ever felt, and somehow, powerful.

'I'm not blind either, Roggero. I think you're a very passionate man. An experienced man. A handsome, sexy man. And perhaps, a man who is bored with what he has. A man who knows what he wants but possibly doesn't know that he can have it.'

He had stared at her, as if he were fighting some internal battle.

She stared back, nervous but excited. She raised her hand and flicked back her long, dark-ginger hair, tilted her head a fraction and bit her lower lip. She was playing a dangerous game and she knew it, but at that precise moment, she simply didn't care. Life in Snowflake Cove was stifling. Boring. She craved excitement. Longed for adventure. Yearned to be loved.

'What are you saying, Severine? Are you saying you want something to happen between us?'

Lines formed around his intense, dark eyes and he scanned her face as if trying to read her mind. Trying to be certain of her intentions. He took her hand and pulled her close.

She should have pushed him away. Told him that this couldn't happen. Run from him and never looked back. Instead she merely nodded.

'Are you sure that's what you want?'

'Oh yes, Roggero. I'm sure it's what I want.'

He led her to the rocky cliff walls of one of the secluded inlets of Snowflake Cove and pressed his hard body against hers; whispered things in her ear the like of which she had never heard. He would stop if she asked him to, but she couldn't find the words. Her breath came in gasps, her mind raced, her mouth and her body responded to his, even though, in her head, an annoying little voice was telling her she mustn't. Telling her this was wrong. But she wanted him. Wanted this. Wanted to be wanted. Wanted to be loved.

That was a night she would never forget because that was the night she tossed aside her childish crush on Logan Dorset, and fell in love with someone else's man.

There were many nights on the beach after that – until the one when she had told him she was pregnant. That was the last night she had lain eyes on Roggero Tazzeone, and now he was back. Back in Snowflake Cove, staying at Snowflake Inn and getting to know their daughter. A daughter he hadn't given a damn about for the entire fifteen years of her life so far.

The metal-against-metal-creak of the back doors of the van made Severine jump. She inhaled deeply, dismissed all thoughts of the past, and twisted in her seat to face Logan.

'I found a blanket.'

24

'So I see.' He didn't look at her. 'Would you mind turning the heater down? It's like a furnace in here and limp lettuce is not a good look, not to mention what heat will do to these oysters.'

'Sorry. I was just so cold. I'm fine now though.' She leant forward and adjusted the heater.

'I'm so pleased.'

He didn't sound pleased; he sounded cross, and he took more than ten minutes to shift the various crates, boxes and bags to fit everything in. When he finally climbed into the driver's seat, his face was flushed and there was a definite scowl on his lips.

'Thanks for the help.'

'Don't take that tone with me, Logan. If you'd wanted my help you should've asked for it. I'm not a mind-reader. And that was the longest five minutes I've ever known. I could've ordered a minicab and been sitting in front of the fire by now.'

He shot her a look, opened his mouth but quickly shut it again and, shaking his head, clicked his seatbelt in place and sped towards Snowflake Cove and her parents' inn.

Neither spoke another word, which was probably just as well, given that Severine was feeling rather emotional.

Chapter Six

Luna got out of the minicab and smiled. Her uncle, Mason Riley was waiting just inside the open doorway of Bell Cottage, leaning on a pair of crutches. He'd told her on the phone a week ago that he'd slipped on the ice and hurt his ankle. It wasn't serious, he'd said, and he didn't look in pain but at his age, injuries often took longer to mend. In a strange way, his fall had reinforced Luna's belief that she had made the right decision and that she could help her uncle just as much as he had helped her in offering her a new start by moving in with him.

'Hello, Mason. You were right about the cold.' She shivered dramatically and grinned as the driver took her cases from the boot. 'I should've taken more notice. Please don't stand there freezing. Go inside.'

'I'm fine, sweetheart.' He beamed at her, gave a little bow and waved one agile hand as if his fingers still danced on the keys of a concert piano. 'Your uncle is always right.' He met her eyes and winked. 'You're looking well. And I'm sure you're even prettier than the last time I saw you. But it's been so long. Come in, come in and let's get you settled.'

The driver helped Luna with her bags and Mason paid him, giving him such a generous tip that the man insisted on taking the cases inside. He placed them to the left of the stairs.

'I leaves here? Is okay? Many thank yous. Enjoy your stays.'

Luna nodded. 'That's perfect, thank you.'

Mason closed the door the moment the driver stepped outside, leaning his back against the wood as if he thought the howling, bitter wind might blow the door open again.

'I think the weather's getting worse. Would you like some tea? Or something stronger? Are you hungry? I'd like to give you a hug, but if I let go of these I may well fall over.' He nodded at his crutches.

Luna hugged him, kissing his cheek. 'I'm so happy to be here. Thank you so much for suggesting this.'

'I'm glad you decided to take me up on the offer. It'll be good for both of us, I'm sure.'

Luna looked him in the eye. 'It'll definitely be good for me and I'll do my best to make sure it's good for you. It'll be such bliss to be able to devote more time to my photography and paintings and sheer heaven not to have to work as a waitress ever again. I hope. I need to find out if I really can make a living from my pictures. Life is too short to put your dreams on hold. That's what Mum always said, didn't she?'

Mason nodded, his eyes brimming with affection and pride. 'She would be so proud of you, sweetheart. I'm proud of you. Things haven't been easy, I know, but you're here now and the future will be better. I'm certain of that.'

'I still can't believe it's been two years since she died. And Dad's been gone for almost four. Sometimes it feels like only yesterday that we were all together, eating, drinking, dancing and generally enjoying life, or all working in that spacious, top floor studio. Little did any of us know what was in store.'

'Not knowing is both a blessing and a curse. Would knowing that those we love will leave us long before they should, make it better or worse, I wonder. You've had such a lot of sadness in these last few years.'

Luna nodded. 'I just wish I'd handled it better. Done things differently. But I can't turn back the clock and I've beaten myself up about it so many times that if thoughts were fists, I'd be back and blue all over.'

'You mustn't punish yourself for the way things turned out. It wasn't your fault. You were vulnerable and you've got a kind, unquestioning heart – just like your dear mother. But everything will be better from now on. I promise you that, sweetheart. All the pain is behind you now.'

Luna nodded. 'Selling the house was difficult, but I think in a way, it's made me feel that this really is a fresh start. A completely new life. I kept picturing Dad sitting at his easel, and me sitting to one side of him, both of us surrounded by paints, whilst Mum was on the other side of the room, her hands covered in plaster or clay, the heady fragrance of Dama de Noche wafting in on the evening breeze through the permanently-open window…' Luna's voice trailed off.

'Dama de Noche – Lady of the Night. She did love the scent of Jasmine. Perhaps because it was her namesake. I should have come and helped you. But I believed you when you said you'd be fine, and I thought you had … had other help.' Mason coughed and fidgeted on his crutches.

Luna smiled wanly. Mason had stopped himself before mentioning Mateus by name and she was grateful. He was the last person she wanted to talk about right now.

'It was something I needed to do by myself. And it was made a lot easier by knowing I was coming here. Anyway, I mustn't get all maudlin.'

'No, indeed. And we'll have plenty of time to chat. There's a roaring fire in the sitting room. Let's go and get you warm.' The crutches squeaked and clicked as he made his way along the hall. 'I feel so useless. I can't wait until I'm able to get about. It does have its advantages though.'

Luna followed behind. 'Oh?'

He stopped at the door to the sitting room, turned and smiled. 'Do you remember I told you about my delightful neighbour, Jane? Jane Dorset. I've been trying to get her to spend a little more time with me but she's been rather stand-offish. I think she's playing hard-to-get, and her daughter-in-law and grandson were staying with her over the holidays. The grandson's still here. But since I had my fall, Jane's been popping in several times a day. She says it's just the neighbourly thing to do, but I think she's really as keen on me as I am on her. She simply won't admit it.' He chuckled and tapped the tip of his long, aquiline nose with one slim finger.

'Mason! You sly devil. That's wonderful news. But … won't I be in the way? Living here I mean. I don't want to cramp your style.'

'You'd never be in the way, sweetheart. Besides, there's always her place. Logan – that's her grandson. I'm sure I've mentioned him before. Anyway, Logan has his hands full. His father died many years ago but Logan has only recently come into his inheritance and Jane has also given him some money. The lad is opening a restaurant in Michaelmas Bay. Tonight, in fact. Everyone in Snowflake Cove and some of the Michaelmas Bay VIPs have been invited to the party. I can't go like this, of course, but you should go in my place. I'll mention it to Jane this morning.'

'Erm … Thanks, Mason, but I'm not sure that I'm up to partying tonight. Besides, I don't want to leave you all alone on my first night here.'

'I'll be fine on my own, but if you'd rather not go, that's your choice. We'll discuss it over a pot of tea.'

Luna smiled. 'I'll put the kettle on.' She glanced towards what was obviously the kitchen. 'You go and sit down.'

Hobbling into the sitting room, Mason called out: 'How was your journey? I forgot to ask.'

Luna filled the kettle and switched it on, then went to the sitting room and popped her head round the door.

'It was fine. Except my flight was late arriving and I had to run for the train. I leapt in just as the doors were closing and got one of my cases caught. So that was fun. Then the train pulled away as I was trying to get my bags stowed on the rack and I managed to fall on to the lap of an unsuspecting man. And I'd already run over his foot with my cases. He wasn't very happy and he moved seats. But it gave Severine and me a conversation starter. I wish she'd told me she was getting off in Michaelmas Bay. It would—'

'Severine? Did you say Severine was on your train? Severine Starr?' He looked surprised.

Luna nodded. 'She didn't give me her surname but yes, her name was Severine. It's a pretty unusual name. Oh! Is she the sister? The one who lives in London. I remember you telling me about the Starrs. They own the inn opposite, don't they?'

He sat forward in his chair and nodded, his eyes as bright and eager as a schoolboy's.

'That's right. I can't recall how much I told you about the family but there have been more than a few revelations over Christmas. I'll fill you in with it all but first, what did Severine say?'

'I don't know why you're so excited but you'll have to wait five minutes whilst I'll get the tea and then we can have a lovely, long gossip.'

Mason harrumphed loudly and folded his arms across his chest, but they grinned mischievously at one another before Luna returned to the kitchen. He would probably be disappointed when she told him, because the truth was, Severine didn't actually say very much. Not about herself. She did repeatedly say how wonderful her fiancé, Harvey was and how she'd had to postpone her wedding due to family commitments, but that she couldn't wait to marry him as soon as she returned to New York. Luna had wondered for a moment whether Severine was trying to convince herself how much she loved the man, or whether she loved him so much that she simply couldn't stop saying it. Severine hadn't mentioned that her family owned Snowflake Inn. Which was a bit odd now that Luna knew who she was. It was as if Severine had wanted to keep it all a secret. And that was rather weird.

Chapter Seven

Logan pulled up beside the old wooden bridge linking Snowflake Isle – and Snowflake Inn – to the mainland.

He and Severine hadn't spoken since they'd left the station. Severine had closed her eyes and pretended she was asleep, which had suited him fine. Except he couldn't stop himself from shooting a couple of glances at her. Maybe more than a couple, if he were honest. Even now, as he took in the curve of her full lips and the dark lashes resting against her rose-coloured cheeks, she didn't open her eyes. Bundled up with the collar of her coat and a thick scarf around her neck, her arms crossed in front of her and her shoulders oddly hunched, she looked like a wax image of herself. Perhaps she actually was asleep. She had said she was exhausted.

'We're here, Severine.' He gently touched her arm but soon wished he hadn't as she glared at him with an angry look in those gorgeous, hazel eyes.

'Thank God for that. It's freezing in here. I can hardly feel my feet.'

'Sorry. I don't think it's that cold, but I wanted to keep it cool so that the ice around the oysters doesn't melt. Do you want me to give you a hand with your luggage? Or are you going to phone your dad and get him to bring the carriage?'

Severine screwed up her pretty nose. 'I'd die from cold by the time he got that horse and cart contraption ready. If you could leave your precious oysters for just five minutes to give me a hand, that would be great.' She shoved open the door and got out.

'Your wish is my command.'

He smiled wanly in spite of the way she was behaving. What the hell did he see in her? She was bad-tempered. Selfish. Demanding.

She was complicated. Beautiful. Sexy as hell.

He sighed as he got out and went to the back of the van. He had already rearranged Severine's luggage at the station so that it was as easy to get to as possible but it still took him several seconds during which Severine stomped her feet as if they were frozen and clapped her gloved-hands together. Anyone would think they were in the arctic. It was cold but it wasn't that unbearable. He pulled up the handles on her cases and nodded forward.

34

'After you.'

A sudden and completely unexpected smile swept across her face and it was as if the clouds had parted and the sun had come out.

'Thank you, Logan. I'm sorry if I'm being a bit of a cow. I'm simply exhausted. And a little anxious about seeing that lot, as you can no doubt imagine.' She tipped her head in the direction of the inn. 'I'm looking forward to seeing Raven of course, but as for the rest of them. The sooner I can leave, the better.'

He smiled back. 'But your family are all so nice. I know you always used to feel as if you were the odd one out, but surely that's not the case now. They've been nothing but kind and helpful to me.'

'How lovely for you. You don't know them as I do. And you weren't around when I told them I was expecting Raven. All these years, they've made me feel as if I had let them down. Evie, of course, can do no wrong, but me. Everything I do is just another screw up as far as they're concerned.'

'Are you sure you're not misjudging them? Perhaps, deep down, it's you who feels you've let them down and …' Her smile turned into a frown and now she was positively glowering at him. He had better shut up before she really lost her temper. 'Sorry. None of my business.'

'It's not me, Logan. It's them. You should've heard the lecture they gave me when I didn't come back for New Year. And then there was all that business about Raven's schooling. I was going to say that Raven was still in shock from the accident and wasn't ready to go back, but no. They insisted we couldn't lie about such things, and if I wasn't coming back and taking Raven home to London, I had to inform her school that she was going to be home-schooled by Mum. Can you believe that? You have no idea of the forms I had to fill in to sort that out.' She stopped suddenly and ran a gloved-hand across her forehead. 'But you're right about one thing. It isn't any of your business. I shouldn't have mentioned it.'

She marched off, leaving him to follow behind with her luggage.

What a wonderful day this was turning into.

Just as he was about to step on to the bridge he heard his name.

'Logan! What are you doing here? I thought you were busy with the restaurant.'

Logan turned and smiled. 'Hello Gran. I am. But I met someone I know at the station. They were coming to Snowflake Inn so I offered to give them a lift.'

He didn't mention Severine's name because he knew that if he did, his gran would be rushing over the bridge to catch her up and would fire a dozen questions at her, one after another. He glanced in Severine's direction and wasn't the least surprised to see she had picked up speed. She was almost on the other side of the bridge and although she could, without a shadow of doubt, hear his gran's booming tones, Severine was clearly pretending she couldn't and had buried her face deeper into her upturned collar, and her scarf.

'Oh. Anyone I know?' Jane asked, peering at Severine's rapidly retreating figure.

'I'll pop in for a very brief chat when I've taken these cases over. Can't stay long, mind you. I've got oysters in the van.' He stepped on to the bridge.

'For tonight? How divine. I was popping next door to Mason's but that can wait. I'll put the kettle on.'

He glanced back over his shoulder. 'You go to Mason's, Gran. I'll nip in and say hello to you both.'

That was a bit of luck. Mason and his gran would no doubt enjoy gossiping about Severine when he told them she was here. At least at Mason's he could make his excuses and leave them to it. If he had had to go to his gran's, he'd be lucky to make an escape this side of lunch time.

He covered the distance between himself and Severine in a matter of seconds.

'I take it you're avoiding my gran.'

She peeped over her collar. 'I'm avoiding everyone I can. Don't take it personally.'

'I'll try not to. And I'm sure Gran will understand and won't try to pry.'

Their eyes met and Severine grinned. 'Jane Dorset. Really? She must have changed one hell of a lot since I last saw her.'

Logan grinned back. 'Nope. She hasn't changed a bit.'

Severine glanced towards the row of cottages sitting across from the isle and opposite Snowflake Inn. 'She's still watching.'

'I'm sure she is. I'll get the third degree when I nip in to say hello.'

'So you've got time to stop for coffee with your gran? What about your precious oysters?'

'I'm not stopping for coffee. I'm merely saying hello.'

'You said hello when she saw you. Do you need to say it twice?'

'Does it matter? You don't care about me or my oysters so what's the problem?'

She scowled at him. 'No problem. I just can't believe you made so much fuss about them and yet you don't seem so bothered now. But I suppose your gran is much more important to you than I am.'

'She's my gran, Severine, and I'm living in her house. But where did that come from? You haven't seen me for more than fifteen years. Please don't pretend you care about what – or who – is important to me, because we both know you don't.'

Severine coughed and flicked her hair from beneath her collar. 'Of course I don't care. I'm simply making a point, that's all.' She pulled open one of the heavy, ancient doors of Snowflake Inn, with ease. 'At least the hinges have been fixed, I see. You can leave my luggage in reception. They've got a porter now I hear.'

'Yes, ma'am. Whatever you say, ma'am.' He walked into reception and placed her bags to one side of the desk.

'Sarcasm doesn't suit you, Logan. Don't let anyone tell you it does. Thanks for the lift and the help with my bags. I suppose I'll see you around.'

She turned to walk towards the kitchen where Logan knew her family would be seated around the table, laughing and chatting and drinking coffee. He wanted to go with her; to offer his support, but that was out of the question. Besides, he had his oysters to think about.

'Severine.'

She stopped and swivelled round to look at him. 'What?'

'Um. I don't suppose you're interested but I'm having a little opening party at my restaurant tonight. It's in Michaelmas Bay. I believe your family will be coming. Please feel free to join them. If you want.'

'*Your* restaurant? But ... don't you work here?'

He shook his head. 'I helped out over Christmas and stayed until your parents employed a full-time chef. I don't expect you'll remember but Dad left me some money and I've just come into that inheritance. I've always wanted a restaurant of my own and one became vacant just before New Year. Gran also gave me some money, so I took the plunge and signed a five-year lease.'

She seemed surprised. 'I had no idea. So are you rich?'

'Would you be interested in me if I were?'

She grinned. 'I might be. Seriously Logan. Good for you. I wish you lots of luck. I'd love to come to the party. Oh. Will everyone else from Snowflake Cove be there?'

'I've invited everyone.'

'In that case … probably not. But thanks.'

'Oh come on, Severine. You're going to have to face them all at some point. They'll all be piling in here the minute they find out you're back. Why not show them you don't care what they think or what they say? You always loved a party.'

She tilted her head. 'That was a long time ago. I've grown up a lot since then. Besides.' She ran a hand over her tummy. 'You seem to have forgotten. I'm pregnant, Logan.'

For one brief moment, he had.

'Severine!' He recognised Jessie Starr's voice – and so did Severine by the expression of dread on her face. 'Good grief girl. Is that you? Have you finally deigned to honour us with your presence? Molly! John! Evie! Get out here this minute. The fatted calf has returned.'

Severine tutted loudly as Jessie appeared from the lounge. 'I think you mean the prodigal daughter has returned, bring out the fatted calf, Gran.'

Jessie screwed up her eyes and smirked. 'No I don't. I meant exactly what I said. Logan? What are you doing here? Don't you have a party to prepare for?'

'I'm leaving now. Lovely to see you, Jessie.' He smiled at Severine. 'Good luck, Severine. It is really good to see you again. I hope I'll see you tonight.'

He hurried towards the door and closed it just as a cacophony of voices flooded into the reception, no doubt giving Severine the welcome she was hoping. Or possibly not.

Chapter Eight

Mason rubbed his chin. 'So Severine didn't mention that she was a Starr, or that she was coming home to see her family?'

Luna shook her head. She had told Mason the few things Severine had said during the train journey. 'Not once. She didn't mention her daughter either. Didn't you say that something happened over the holidays?'

Mason was about to reply when the sing-song sound of the doorbell made his eyes light up and a huge smile spread across his face.

'That'll be Jane. Would you let her in please, sweetheart?'

'Of course.'

Luna walked into the hall and opened the front door to an elegant-looking woman who was probably in her eighties. The woman was smiling broadly at first, but looked a little taken aback to see someone other than Mason standing before her. Then the penny clearly dropped.

'Oh, hello. You must be Luna. Mason's niece. I completely forgot you were arriving today. I'm Jane. A friend of your uncle. It's lovely to meet you, dear. I've heard so much about you I feel as if we're already friends. I hope we shall be.'

So this was Jane Dorset. The woman Mason had a thing for.

'Hello Jane. I hope so too. Please come in.'

Jane stepped into the hall and walked towards the sitting room whilst Luna closed the door.

'I hope you and Mason don't mind but my grandson is going to pop his head in briefly. He can't stay because of the oysters but at least he'll say hello. Mason, it's me. Your niece is simply lovely.' She beamed at Luna and joined Mason in front of the fire, sitting on the chair Luna had vacated.

Luna smiled and collected the tea tray. She had no idea what Jane meant about the oysters but it probably didn't matter.

'I'll make some fresh. Would you prefer tea or coffee, Jane? And is your grandson joining us right away?'

'Coffee for me please. Nice and milky. Logan will be here any minute. He's just helping someone staying at Snowflake Inn, with their luggage.'

Mason leant forward and tapped Jane's knee. 'And you'll never guess who that is.' He grinned mischievously. 'None other than Severine.'

Jane's mouth formed a perfect 'O' as Luna left them to it.

From the kitchen, Luna could hear her uncle and Jane gossiping about Severine. He was telling Jane about the train journey, not that there was much to tell, and Jane was making 'ooh-ing' and 'ah-ing' responses to every word he said.

Luna put the kettle on and leant against the worktop, waiting for it to boil, her mind drifting back to thoughts of Spain, and Mateus, her ex-boyfriend.

What would he make of Snowflake Cove? He'd no doubt hate it. Especially the gossip. That was what he disliked the most about the village where they'd lived. The village he had been so desperate to leave.

She straightened her back and clenched her teeth.

Without the gossips, would she ever have discovered his deception? It had taken long enough even so. Usually, that sort of juicy titbit would have spread around the village faster than the summer wildfires in the hills beyond, but his affair had been going on for at least a year before she finally found out. And she had only found out after he had left.

She sneered at her silhouette on the glossy surface of the wall cupboard opposite.

How could she have been so stupid? Why hadn't anyone in the village warned her? Was it because she was still getting over the loss of her mum, just a couple of years after losing her dad? Perhaps they all thought she was too fragile to cope. Perhaps they thought the affair was just a passing fancy. Once Mateus had gone – and taken every last bit of the cash Luna kept in the house, with him, and the money in their joint bank account – the villagers all rallied round. They all said they hadn't had the heart to tell her. Didn't want to see her hurt again.

Well that worked out well, didn't it?

She shook her head at her own foolishness. Mateus had repeatedly told her he wanted to leave the village. To go to Madrid, or Paris, or London. Any big city would clearly suffice. Perhaps if she'd sold the house sooner and said yes, he wouldn't have looked elsewhere for his ticket out of there.

Was that all she had been? A sort of meal ticket with free bed and board until someone else came along and offered him something better. They had met at her mum's funeral. Like her mother, Jasmine Blake, Mateus Ruiz was a struggling sculptor who had said that he admired Jasmine's work and hoped one day to be half as good as she was. Was that just a line? A way to wheedle himself into Luna's affections. It had worked, hadn't it? Less than a month after the funeral, Mateus and Luna were living together in her parents' house. But he didn't seem to spend much time working clay with his agile hands.

'Luna, sweetheart.' Mason's voice, the whistling kettle and the chime of the doorbell all sang out in unison.

'I'll get it.' She pushed herself away from the worktop, took the kettle off the stove and headed to the door.

'Oh. Hello.' The man from the station sounded surprised but a smile crept into his eyes.

'It's you!' He wasn't as surprised as Luna.

'Me? Um. Have we met? I'm sorry but I'm terrible with faces.'

'Yes. I mean, no. Not exactly. I arrived by train this morning with Severine. I saw you at the station when you came to meet her.'

'Came to meet her? Do you know Severine? Did you say you were at the station? I didn't see you. She didn't say she was travelling with a friend. How did you get here?'

'Minicab. Mason had ordered one to meet me. And I'm not Severine's friend. We met on the train. I saw you talking to her when I passed by on the concourse.'

'Logan?' Jane called out. 'Is that you?'

Logan pulled a face and grinned. 'It's me, Gran.'

Luna quickly stepped aside, shaking her head and laughing as she did so.

'I'm so sorry. Please come in. I'm Luna. Mason's niece.'

He studied her face for a second, smiling. 'Hi Luna. I'm Logan. Jane Dorset's grandson.'

'Are you Severine's boyfriend?'

Where on earth had that come from? Luna bit her lip.

Logan drew his brows together in a deep frown. 'No. Just a friend. A friend who happened to be in the right place at the right time. Or wrong place, depending on how you look at it.'

'Sorry? I don't understand.'

Logan sighed. 'Believe me. Nor do I.' He shook his head. 'Are they in the sitting room?'

'Oh yes. I'm making coffee. Would you like some? Or tea, if you prefer. Do go through.'

'After you.' He followed Luna along the hall. 'Thanks for the offer but I really can't stay. I've got a few crates of oysters in my van and although they're encased in ice, it won't be too much longer before that melts – even in this weather.'

She grinned at him over her shoulder. 'Ah. That explains the oysters.'

'Sorry?'

She stopped at the kitchen door and laughed. 'Jane said that you couldn't stay for long because of the oysters. Now I know what she meant.'

'Those oysters have a lot to answer for.' He turned at the sitting room doorway. 'Um. Did Gran mention I'm having a party tonight? Everyone from this village will be there – and some posh-knobs from Michaelmas Bay. You're welcome to join us. It's an opening party for my restaurant.'

'Thanks. That's really kind of you. Jane's only just arrived so she hasn't mentioned it yet, but Mason did. You must be so excited. It's a wonderful achievement.'

'It's not much of an achievement yet. Just took over from the previous owner. But I am excited and I want to do a lot with it once it's up and running. All I've done so far is have the place redecorated and new equipment, tables and chairs installed.'

'And purchased oysters. Don't forget those.'

Amusement danced in his eyes. 'Ah yes. The oysters. Probably developing life-threatening bacteria as we speak.'

'Remind me to avoid the oysters tonight then.'

Logan grinned. 'I'm cooking some and adding burnt butter. Stick to those and you'll be fine.'

'Is burnt butter a gastronomic delicacy or are you expecting some disasters in the kitchen?'

Luna's cheeks flushed. The butter would easily burn if he looked at it the way he was now looking at her, with that wicked grin on his perfect mouth and that spark of heat in his eyes as he gave a quick burst of laughter.

'A bit of both.' His voice sounded a little huskier than it had.

'What are you two laughing about?' Mason called from the sitting room.

Logan glanced over his shoulder. 'Oysters, Mason.' He smiled back at Luna. 'I really hope

48

you'll come tonight.' Then he turned and walked towards Jane. 'I can't stay, Gran.'

He bent and kissed her cheek as Luna watched him from the hall.

'So you're not going to tell me about Severine, then?' Jane sounded disappointed.

'Nothing to tell, Gran. I bumped into her at the station. Gave her a lift. Helped her across the bridge with her luggage. End of story.'

'What did you talk about on the way?'

'We didn't. She was tired and she nodded off.'

'That's a likely tale.' Jane gave him an affectionate poke with her finger.

'Sadly, it's the truth.'

He looked back at Luna and, having been caught ogling him, she dashed into the kitchen and tried to concentrate on making the coffees, but she strained her ears to listen to the ongoing conversation. Or should that be interrogation?

'You're honestly telling us that she didn't say a word?'

'Yes, Gran. Other than that she was cold and tired. Although I think she may have mentioned that she was dreading all the gossip.'

It seemed Jane was determined to extract some snippet of news from Logan, however tiny, and Logan appeared to be equally as determined not to reveal any.

Why was that? Perhaps he was telling the truth. After all, Luna had spent more than an hour on the train with Severine and hadn't any news to tell her uncle. It was highly likely that Logan was in a similar position. Especially as he'd spent less than twenty minutes with Severine.

Jane clearly wasn't giving up and only briefly glanced at Luna as she brought in the tray of coffees. 'I'm surprised. I would have thought she would have chatted away non-stop, catching up on all your news and sharing hers with you. After all, she used to have a bit of a crush on you.'

Jane took the coffee Luna handed her and smiled, but quickly returned her gaze to her grandson, as did Luna, on hearing that statement and the odd guttural sound it extracted from Logan.

'No she didn't! She hardly even knew I existed. It was the other …' His face flushed and his Adam's Apple jittered. 'I mean … she was in love with someone else.'

Jane tutted. 'I meant before she had that unforgivable affair with the father of her sister's best friend. Before Roggero Tazzeone.'

Luna watched Logan's mouth form a tight line before he took a deep breath and replied:

'Severine has never been interested in me. Before or after Roggero. As for unforgivable – we all make mistakes, Gran. Don't we all deserve a second chance?'

Jane shrugged. 'There are mistakes and there are mistaken ideas. Severine knew exactly what she was doing. Mark my words. That girl never does anything by mistake.'

He tensed visibly and clenched his fists. 'I've got to go. See you all tonight.'

Before anyone had a chance to reply, he was gone. And from the loud bang echoing down the hall, he must have closed the front door with a bit too much force.

Chapter Nine

Severine was already wishing she had merely sent her daughter an open-dated plane ticket and told her to join them in New York whenever she was ready to make the move. Life would have been so much easier.

But she hadn't, and now she was sitting at the kitchen table in Snowflake Inn trying to think of a way to disappear to whichever room her parents had allocated her – and she had been with them for less than ten minutes.

Perhaps if Raven had been there, it would have been a little better, but Raven was out with Roggero, her father or so Jessie had said.

Her father.

Those were two words Severine had been trying not to associate with Raven for the past fifteen years.

Obviously the topic had come up. Several times in fact over the years, especially when Raven

52

reached her teens. But Severine had been lying to everyone else about *that man* for so long that lying to her daughter seemed the most natural – and definitely the simplest – thing to do.

She'd told Raven she had no idea where Raven's father was. (That much was true at least.) That he was just a man she had met at the Michaelmas Bay fair. (A lie) That she had had a fling and hey presto – Raven was conceived. Severine had said the father didn't know about the pregnancy. (Also a lie.) And that she had no way of getting in touch with him. (Only partly true.) Sylvie, Roggero's wife in all but name, might have had some idea where her cheating partner had gone – although there were rumours that Sylvie had buried him in the garden because, despite them living together for years and having two children, he had never put a ring on her finger and wasn't ever likely to. But as the poor woman seemed as surprised as everyone else that the man had simply disappeared, Severine seriously doubted that. Besides, how could Severine have asked? She could hardly have knocked on Sylvie's front door and said, 'Excuse me. Do you know where Roggero is? Only I'm expecting his child. He had a bit of a strop when I told him and I haven't seen him since.'

No one other than herself and Roggero knew of their affair.

Oh, apart from Logan Dorset.

For some stupid reason she had been foolish enough to blurt it all out to him and cry on his shoulder, the night she heard Roggero had vanished.

That had been an awful night. For her and for Logan. She heard the news that her lover had disappeared, and she had a distinct feeling she might never see him again. As she wept in Logan's arms, her dad appeared, and Logan got the news that his own father had died, suddenly and somewhat unexpectedly it seemed; he had succumbed to the cancer that had riddled his body for some time.

'Well, child.' Jessie gave Severine's hand a gentle slap. 'What have you got to say for yourself?'

Severine glared at her. 'I've had a long journey and, as my daughter isn't here, I'd like to go and lie down until she returns.'

'That's it? No apology. No explanation. You haven't even said you're pleased to be here.'

'Why is that, I wonder, Gran?' Severine sucked in a breath. 'I don't think I have anything to apologise for. It's not my fault the weather was so dreadful. Delaying seemed the sensible thing to do … in my condition.' She placed a hand on her tummy.

'Oh don't give me that twaddle. I wasn't born with the fairies. If you'd wanted to come home, you would have. You and I both know that.'

'Jessie.' Severine's mum, Molly intervened, her voice soft and soothing. 'Don't you think you're possibly being a little harsh? I was as cross as you are, but the important thing is that she's home now. There's no point in raking over the past. It's the future that's important.'

'Bah! Whose future? Did she think about Raven's future when she ran off to America with a man she hardly knows? When she phoned us – *phoned us mind* – to tell us she was getting married? When she blurted out that she was expecting. And moving thousands of miles away.'

'I agree it would've been better to break all that news in person.' Molly squeezed one of Severine's hands as Severine tapped her fingers on the table in an irritated fashion. 'But we all know Severine acts … hastily. I'm sure she didn't mean any harm by it. Did you darling?'

Severine returned her mum's smile, though with less enthusiasm than Molly.

'Of course I didn't. If I'd known you were going to act as if I was trying to blow up the inn and everyone in it, I'd have waited. I was just so excited. Haven't any of you been that excited about something? So much so that if you don't tell the people who are supposed to love you, your news, you think you're going to burst. That's how I felt. I wanted you all to know. And you all behaved as if I said I'd contracted the plague or something.'

Evie – who had been making coffee for everyone – thumped a mug on the table in front of her sister.

'No we didn't, Severine. That's unfair. We were all thrilled you're in love. We all want you to be happy, believe me. We know what you're like when you're not. Don't scowl at me. The days of me keeping my mouth shut are long gone. What upset us all, was the way you told us. I wasn't here when you called and I came in to find Raven in tears. Mum more upset that I've seen her in years. Dad almost unable to speak. And Gran. Well...' She threw Jessie a little smile across the table. 'You can imagine how Gran felt. All we're saying is we think the least you could do is see things from this side of the pond. I mean, why the sudden move to New York, for instance?'

'Why the...?' Severine shook her head in exasperation. 'Because I think it would be rather nice to actually live with the man I'm about to marry, Evie. That's why. I bet if Zachary Thorn asked you to move to Outer Mongolia, or the Moon, you'd go.'

Evie's face glowed at the mention of her boyfriend's name and she beamed at Severine.

'You're right. I would. But I'd tell my family in person. And if I had a teenage daughter, I'd talk to her about it first. And I'd make damn sure that she was happy about it because if she wasn't, as much as I love Zachary, he'd be living on his own until we figured out something else.'

'Yes, well. You always were the goody-two-shoes, weren't you? If I'm such a bad mother, Raven's probably better off staying here. That's what she said she's wants. Of course that was before her errant father bloody well showed up and threw a spanner in the works.'

'Can you hear yourself?' Jessie said, banging her mug on the table top. 'And that's another thing. Roggero Tazzeone! Surely you realise we deserve a bit of an explanation about that sordid little affair.'

Severine got to her feet, her chair tipping back on to the floor with a resounding thud.

'It wasn't sordid. We were in love! At least I was. He said he was, too. He was even talking about leaving Sylvie and the kids – until I told him I was pregnant. You may not care – and I don't suppose for one minute you do. That any of you do. But that man broke my heart. Thoroughly, utterly and completely. I actually thought it would never mend. That I'd never find love or happiness again. And then I met Harvey and fell head over heels. *Forgive me* if I didn't stop to wonder if my *loving* family would prefer me not to be happy.'

'That's enough, Severine!' Her father, John banged his hand flat on the table. 'Pick up that chair and sit yourself down. I'm not sure how things got this crazy but there are some things I am sure about and I'm going to say them without anyone interrupting me.'

John rarely lost his temper but his bright red cheeks, the set of his jaw and the way he was clenching his mug made it clear this was one of those rare occasions. Severine hesitated for less than five seconds and everyone in the room fell silent until she put her chair back in place and resumed her seat.

John nodded and took a deep breath, as if he was trying hard to calm himself.

'You've lied to this family for the last sixteen years, Severine. From the minute you told us you were pregnant by someone who worked at the fair. When we found out the truth at Christmas, it was as if you'd stuck knives in all our hearts. Molly's and mine in particular. We're your parents and we love you. We've always loved you. We will try to support anything you do. We always have. To not tell us about Roggero made us feel we'd failed as your parents. It hurt. It still hurts. And let's not forget, he and Sylvie were our friends. Their daughter was, and still is, Evie's best friend. Their son is working here part-time. Imagine how that news made us feel. Made them feel. But we support you nonetheless. We love you in spite of the lie. We simply want you to talk to us about it. About your choices now, too. We want you to be happy. We want you to know that you can tell us anything and we will always support you. Always love you. Always want, more than anything in the world, for you to be happy. But we also want that for Raven. And the thought of moving to New

York is not making her happy, Severine. Especially now. Whether you like it or not, Roggero is here and he genuinely wants to get to know his daughter. He seems truly sorry for the past. I have no idea where we all go from here, but please stop trying to fight us. Stop accusing us of not caring about you or your happiness. Because I can assure you, my darling, we do care. Possibly more than you could ever know.' He coughed lightly. 'There. I've said my piece. Why don't you go and have a lie down? The inn is full and we didn't know you were coming until yesterday, so you're sharing Evie's room, just like you did as children. Your mum will make a hearty lunch and when it's ready, we'll call you and we'll all sit around this table and eat and chat, like the loving, happy family we are, deep down. Now go. And I don't word to hear a word from anybody. No, Mum.' He glared at Jessie. 'Not even from you.'

Chapter Ten

Roggero Tazzeone watched his three children as they searched the evening and partywear section of the department store for something new to wear to Logan Dorset's party that night. They were laughing, joking, teasing him and one another, and so far, were having the perfect day out shopping. He was treating them and had told them they could have whatever they liked, to which Raven had replied, 'That's pretty much everything in the store then.' Roland had asked if he could have a new car instead and Juniper said she'd need to make a list and get back to him.

Roggero turned to them, laughing. 'Anything in this department. To wear to the party. And perhaps one other thing each if you are all very well-behaved.'

'Not much chance of that,' said Roland, with a mischievous grin.

'Hmm. That's gonna be tough,' Raven said, trying but failing to look serious. 'I'm not that good at being well-behaved.' She creased her brow. 'Does a skirt and top count as one thing or two?'

'That's what I was going to ask,' added Juniper, grinning and giving her half-sister a playful nudge.

'Me too,' said Roland, winking.

Roggero felt his chest swell with happiness. If anyone had been watching they would never have believed that this was anything other than a 'normal' family. A father and his children out to buy clothes for a special event. If he had harboured any lingering doubt before, he now knew for certain that for once in his life he had made the right decision to return to Michaelmas Bay after all his years away.

Not that he had actually given the matter much thought at the time. When that footage of the accident involving his son – and a daughter he hadn't met – had aired on TVs the world over, it had felt as if the gods were sending him a personal message. "Get your backside off that stool and go and make amends with your children". In that split second, he knew that was exactly what he had to do. What he wanted to do, more than anything in the world.

It had taken him a few minutes to physically get off the stool though. Seeing two of his children rescued from a freezing sea and his other daughter standing, terrified at the edge of the cliff was like watching a disaster movie – and he was glued to the TV. His heart thumped against his chest, his legs felt like lead and his feet, like gelato. He was sure if he stood up, he would fall over, so he sat on the stool at the coffee bar where, every day, he had his *un caffè*. He remained there open-mouthed, gaping at the small screen high on the wall opposite.

He heard himself order a grappa and un caffè doppio (a double espresso) despite the fact that he had just finished the first cup he'd ordered, and knocked both back within seconds. He remembered dialling a number and booking the first flight out of Rome to any London airport. But how he got to Snowflake Inn, or how long it had taken him, he wasn't exactly certain. He spent the entire journey wondering and worrying about the reaction his sudden and unexpected arrival would have on everyone – not just his children.

His former partner, Sylvie was probably married to someone by now. Marriage was what she had always wanted but it was the one thing Roggero wasn't prepared to give her. Their children, Juniper and Roland were adults now and might not welcome his return. Juniper would remember him. She had been in her teens when he left but Roland was a mere child of three. How would they feel, seeing him after almost sixteen years without contact? Angry, hurt, abandoned? Would they have it in their hearts to forgive him?

And what about Raven, the daughter he had never met? How would she feel? Did she even know of his existence?

And then there was his ex-lover, Severine. Had she married? The report of the accident hadn't mentioned her. It had only said that Raven, who had been staying at her grandparents' inn, was taking part in an organised snowball fight, along with her friend Roland and several others when the accident occurred, and Raven and Roland had fallen over the cliff edge. Either the report had been limited on facts, or Raven had no idea that Roland was her brother. Half-brother to be precise. Had Severine kept that from them? And where was she? He would have spotted her stunning face amongst the crowd of onlookers. It would have stood out like a beacon in a storm.

A sudden and horrendous thought dawned on him. Had something happened to Severine?

To his complete surprise that thought was one he could not bear. To never see her face again. Those hazel eyes that burnt like glowing embers when she was cross and gleamed like warm amber when she was happy. And that hair, as soft and glossy as a ginger kitten's … or perhaps a lion cub, would be more apt for memories of Severine. Would he never have a chance to see those pouting lips again? To kiss them into a smile. All he could think about was Severine and his children. His head ached with worry, his heart ached with pain, his body ached from lack of sleep and from sitting for hours on planes and trains and minicab seats.

When he had eventually arrived in Snowflake Cove, everyone was singing carols around the Christmas tree. He had scanned the small crowd for Severine but she wasn't there. He saw Roland, and recognised him immediately. His son was a younger version of himself, like looking at an old photo. And Juniper, who had grown from a skinny teenager into a very pretty woman was the spitting image of her mother Sylvie, with just a hint of Roggero in her looks. Then he had seen Raven. Beautiful, like Severine but with his black hair colour, she was even more stunning in the flesh; he would know her anywhere.

Doubts and anxiety left him, replaced by a burning pride in his children and a fierce determination to protect them from any future harm. He would take whatever they threw at him with humility and repentance. He would give them all the time they might need to let him into their lives. If that took years for a mere fraction, it would be more than he probably deserved. He had the rest of his life to earn their forgiveness, even if he never earnt their love.

But what of Severine? He had held back as long as he could. The Starrs were hurt, disappointed and angry when they realised he was Raven's father. Juniper and Roland were bemused and cross. Raven was astonished, yet strangely happy. Sylvie was … furious. Asking about

Severine had not seemed the wisest thing to do. But eventually he had to ask.

The news had been good and bad.

Severine was alive and well.

She was also engaged, pregnant and about to marry another man.

'Dad? Dad?' Raven gently poked his chest with her finger. She was laughing and smiling at him and wearing a dress that was far too sexy and revealing for a fifteen-year-old. 'Are you day-dreaming? What do you think? I know you're gonna say I'm too young to wear a dress like this, but I'm not, Dad. I'll be sixteen soon. Old enough to have sex, get married and make babies.'

That truth took Roggero's breath away for a second or two, as did the fact that Raven was going to be even more beautiful than her mother, Severine, when she grew to womanhood. But what gave him a lump in his throat was that after only a few short weeks, the daughter he abandoned before she was born was now calling him 'Dad' as if it were the most natural thing in the world. It made his heart fit to explode with delight and without thinking he reached out and hugged her to him, planting a fatherly kiss on the top of her head.

'Get off, Dad.' She laughed into his chest and didn't try to move as she hugged him back. 'You're sooooo embarrassing at times.'

'*Bambina*. I cannot help myself.' He edged her away, smiling and tapped her nose with the tip of his finger. 'The dress, it is beautiful.' He nodded.

'But you, you do not need such a thing. And this red, with your black hair.' Shaking his head, he glanced over to Juniper. 'Juniper. Help me. This colour is not good for Raven, I think. It makes her look much older than she is, no?'

Juniper creased her brows, tipped her head to one side and nodded. 'Sorry, sis, but it drains the colour from your face. I have to agree with DadToo.'

DadToo was the name Juniper and Roland had decided to call Roggero. He was their birth father but Peter Green, the man who had married their mother Sylvie and brought them up as his own, was the man whom they now called Dad. Neither of them wanted to change that and Roggero understood. Sylvie – who still bore Roggero some resentment, although it was diminishing a little every day, had said that she could think of a few things they could call the man who had left them without a word. None of her suggestions were pleasant and a few weren't fit to be repeated. After a considerable amount of discussion, some of which was heated, Juniper, Roland and Sylvie agreed that Roggero would be called, DadToo. Not two as in second, but too, as in also. Juniper and Roland had asked their dad Peter how he felt about it and Peter, being the wonderful man that he was, merely said that whatever they wanted to call Roggero was fine with him. Roggero thanked his lucky stars that after he had left, Sylvie had met and married Peter. It was possibly one of the most sensible things she had ever done, in his opinion.

Raven ran her hand over the tight-fitting red dress and looked a little disappointed.

'Roland? What do you think?'

Her half-brother shrugged. 'It makes you look like a tart. Don't glare at me. You asked for my opinion. I gave it.'

'Thanks a lot.' Raven glanced at Juniper, then at her dad and back again to Juniper. 'Does it? Do I look like a hooker?'

Juniper nodded. 'Yeah. Sorry. You've got a fantastic figure but your boobs are half- hanging out of that.'

Roggero closed his eyes tight for a second. He was still struggling to come to terms with having two daughters, let alone two daughters who openly discussed sex, boobs and other parts of both the female and male anatomy. It was a completely new concept for him – and one he wasn't yet entirely comfortable with.

He cleared his throat. 'I liked the pink dress.'

'Really? The first one I tried on? Don't you think it was a bit too … girly?'

Roggero grinned. 'You are a girl, no? Why is it not a good thing to be one?'

Roland smirked. 'She wants to look like a bad-ass, or a sex-bomb, not a virginal school girl.'

'What makes you so sure I'm a virgin?'

There was a sudden hush throughout the store as Raven's words seemed to bounce off every wall, as if loud speakers boomed them out.

Raven blushed. 'Sorry. That came out louder than I expected.' She lowered her voice. 'I am, Dad. In case you're wondering.' She glanced at him beneath her lashes, clearly seeking his approval. 'I'll go and try on the pink one again.'

'Nice one, sis.' Juniper grinned and nudged Raven's arm as she headed back to the changing room. 'Always good to give the parents something else to occupy their thoughts.'

Whether or not his fifteen-year-old daughter was a virgin was the last thing Roggero was ready to think about. But he was more than a little relieved that she had said she was. He would quite like her to remain that way until she was at least thirty. Sex could bring ecstasy and delight. It could also bring unexpected children. And that wasn't always the wonderful news it should be. He knew from experience it could be devastating, life-changing and ultimately, heart-breaking for everyone concerned.

Chapter Eleven

'Severine. Severine!'

Severine opened her eyes and was startled to see her sister, Evie standing beside the bed, grinning at her. It took several seconds to realise where she was.

'Don't look so horrified,' Evie said. 'Mum sent me up to tell you lunch is ready. She's dishing it up in about five minutes so that's how long you've got if you want to splash some water on your face. And you might want to comb your hair.'

Severine struggled to sit up. Having been awoken from a deep sleep, she was drowsy and muddle-headed. Stifling a yawn, she stretched her arms out either side.

'I was dreaming about Harvey. I thought I was in New York … until I saw your ugly mug.' She grinned up at Evie, who tutted as she turned away.

'Yeah, yeah. You're just jealous.' Evie stopped at the door and nodded. 'It's good to have you back here, despite the fact that you're as unpleasant as ever.'

'Evie?' Severine called after her.

'Yes.'

'Has he …' Severine fiddled with the trim of the duvet. 'Has he changed?'

'Who? Roggero?' Evie walked back towards the bed and sat on the edge. 'In looks, no, not much. He's older of course and he's got a touch of grey at his temple and the sides but he still looks young for his age. And he's as handsome as ever. In personality I'd say he's had a complete transformation. Travelling the world must have done him good. He told us he's been living and working all over the place and had only recently settled in Rome. But now he's looking for a house in Michaelmas Bay. He really wants to make amends to Juniper and Roland. And he genuinely cares about Raven and wants to get to know her.'

'How lovely for him.'

Evie looked her in the eye. 'Are you annoyed that he's still handsome, that he's back, or that he's spending time with his kids?'

Severine jumped up and marched towards the en suite. 'I'm annoyed that he's been traipsing all over the globe whilst I was struggling to bring up his daughter without so much as a word or a penny from him.'

'Yes. Sylvie Green said almost the same thing. And to his face.'

'At least he left Sylvie with the house. He left me with nothing.'

Evie made a choking sound and Severine leant backwards from the sink to get a look at her sister's face.

'What?'

Evie shook her head. Wild, ginger hair danced around her shoulders but the expression on her freckled face was now serious.

'He left you with Raven. She may not have seemed like a gift at the time, but she is. And I hate to point this out, Severine, but Sylvie deserved the house. She deserved a lot more. She'd been paying towards the mortgage and it was the family home they'd been living in for seventeen or so years. Besides, he didn't exactly leave it to her, don't forget. He simply walked out one day and never came back.'

'That's the same thing.'

Evie shook her head again. 'No it's not. It's absolutely not! Sorry. But you know the hell Sylvie went through. She spent enough time here in floods of tears. Even you couldn't help but notice that. Although now that I think about it, you did always seem to disappear whenever she came over with Juniper and Roland. Did you feel guilty? Is that why?'

'I know she was very upset, but it wasn't my fault.'

'Not your fault! How can you say that? You'd been having an affair with the man she loved, Severine.'

'Roggero didn't love her anymore. He said he wasn't sure he ever had. And I was as upset as she was.'

'But she'd built a life with him. Had kids with him. Washed and cooked and cleaned for him. You were having sex with him as if none of that mattered. Although none of us knew that at the time, did we? We only found out at Christmas. That was a surprise, let me tell you. A huge surprise as surprises go. And we had a few of those at Christmas.' Evie folded her arms in front of her. 'You shouldn't have lied about it. You should've told us all the truth. At least Raven deserved to know who her father was. Have you any idea how she felt when he turned up and it all came out? Have you actually talked to her about it?'

'Yes, I've talked to her. Of course I have. But she always cuts me short and says something like, 'Whatever, Mum. We'll discuss it when you come home.' You know what she can be like.'

Evie's mouth fell open. 'What she can …! I don't believe you, Severine. You really haven't changed one iota. I thought that now you were in love and about to get married – and expecting another child – you might have mellowed a bit. That maybe you'd think about someone else before yourself. Try to see things from another person's point of view. But no. You're still the same old Severine.'

'I don't know what you're getting so upset about. You have no idea what it was like. How difficult it was for me. How difficult all this is. You weren't the one who was deserted by the man she loved. He broke my heart, Evie. Now he's back after all these years and trying to play some game of happy families. And I'm expected to be okay with that? I'm the bad guy?'

Evie stood up abruptly. 'He broke Sylvie's heart too. And Juniper's. Roland was too young to understand but … Oh what's the point? I'll see you downstairs. Don't keep us waiting or we'll start without you. You may not have changed, Severine, but things around here most definitely have.'

Severine winced as the door banged shut.

What the hell did Evie mean by that?

Chapter Twelve

Molly smiled lovingly when Severine walked into the kitchen.

'Hello darling. Did you manage to get some sleep? Come and sit here, next to me. It's been so long since I've seen you properly.'

Molly pulled out a chair and stood behind it until Severine sat down. She planted a kiss on the top of Severine's head and squeezed her shoulders. Severine was going to say that it had only been a couple of hours since her mum had seen her, but that would have been facetious. And pointless. She simply smiled at Molly instead.

'This smells delicious, Mum.'

Molly beamed at her and removed the lid from the large, cast iron, casserole pot in the centre of the kitchen table.

'It's your favourite, darling. Cheesy chilli chicken, topped with baked chips.' She ladled several spoonfuls on to Severine's plate.

'A heart attack in a pot,' John said, but his smile showed he loved it as much as Severine did.

Molly tutted before grinning at her husband. 'Give over. There's lots of healthy veg in there, and the chips are homemade, so the only slightly bad thing is the cheese.' She gave him an even larger helping than she had to Severine.

'Nothing wrong with cheese,' Jessie said. 'Men working the fields used to live on bread and cheese. Where d'you think a ploughman's lunch comes from? Full of protein and goodness is cheese.'

Evie grinned. 'And preservatives and other chemicals, these days, Gran. But I love it, so I'm not complaining.'

Molly served herself last and sat down, smiling with contentment. 'It's so lovely to have us all together again. It's just a pity Raven isn't here. What time did she say she'd be back, Evie?'

'Around four, I think.'

'I can't wait to see her,' Severine said, before tucking into her casserole.

'I'm sure she feels the same,' Jessie said. 'And maybe if you'd given us all more notice of your arrival, she would've been here to meet you.'

'It was all very last minute, otherwise I would've. But then I thought it might be a lovely surprise. I texted her the minute I landed. And Mum.'

Jessie nodded. 'Yes. Raven rushed in and told us the second she got your text. As for a surprise.

Didn't it occur to you that we may have had quite enough of those over the holidays? A bit of notice would've been far better.'

'Well, she's here now,' John said, between mouthfuls. 'And Raven will see her soon enough.'

Jessie grinned mischievously. 'And Roggero Tazzeone. I bet you're looking forward to that, aren't you, my girl?'

Severine glared at her gran. 'Roggero Tazzeone means nothing to me. He broke my heart but I eventually got over it. All that matters to me now is Harvey. And Raven of course. And my baby. Which not one of you has even so much as mentioned, by the way. I thought you'd be happy for me.'

'Oh darling!' Molly leapt from her chair and hugged Severine. 'We are. You know we are. And we've talked about you and the baby a lot. We've always asked how things are whenever you've called. We're all so happy for you, and very excited.' She gave her another kiss, this time on her cheek. 'Aren't we, John? Jessie? Evie? We're thrilled to bits, aren't we?'

'Thrilled,' Jessie said, sardonically.

'Of course we are.' John did actually look pleased.

Evie nodded and smiled. 'We are, Severine. Honestly. We're very happy for you.'

A caustic remark came to Severine's lips but something made her hold back and she surprised even herself when all she said was, 'Thank you.'

76

Molly resumed her seat. 'It's a pity Harvey couldn't come with you. It would've been so lovely to meet him.'

'He's really busy getting the house in New York ready for our arrival. But you have met him. You've chatted on Skype.'

'Yes, but that's not the same, darling. It's so much nicer to meet someone in the flesh. Will he be coming over soon to join you?'

'Um.' Was now the time to tell them she wasn't planning on staying here long so there was no need for him to join her? Somehow, she thought not. 'It's difficult for him to get away. But now that we've postponed the wedding, you'll all be coming over for that, won't you? So you'll meet him then.'

'You expect me to get on a plane at my age?' Jessie said. 'Why can't you get married here? You are the bride, after all. Surely he and his family can do the travelling. That seems fair to me.'

'I'm sure it does. But we want to get married at his parents' house. It's so gorgeous there. And huge. They're loaded, you know.'

'We're loaded,' Jessie said. 'Now.'

Evie nodded. 'Thanks to Joshua Thorn.'

'Loaded?' Severine shot rapid looks at everyone around the table and finally back to Jessie. 'I know he gave you an IOU or something for money he owed to you and Grandad but no one said anything about loaded. How much did he give you?'

Jessie glanced at her. 'Nothing more than we deserved.'

'But how much was that?'

Jessie grinned like the proverbial cat. 'One million pounds.'

The clatter of Severine's knife and fork hitting her plate rang out around the kitchen. It took a moment until she was able to speak again.

'One. Million. Pounds! Are you serious?' Her eyes darted at everyone. 'Why the hell didn't anyone tell me?'

'Don't get cross, darling.' Molly squeezed Severine's hand, a worried expression on her face. 'It's not the sort of thing one talks about over the phone.'

'Not the ... Why the hell not? We talk about everything else. You all had no problem telling me how you felt about my intended marriage. Or Harvey. Or the fact that you all thought I should've been here, not there. No problem talking about my life choices, or that you felt my daughter might want to remain here with you and not come with me – her own mother – to New York. No problem insisting that I contact Raven's school and get her home-schooled here. And you definitely had no problem talking about how angry, hurt and disappointed you all were in me when Roggero turned up. But telling me we're now rich and we never have to worry about money again for the rest of our lives isn't something you think you can talk about over the phone!'

'Severine.' John's tone held a note of warning.

'Well actually, it's Gran's money,' Evie said. 'Not ours. So Gran's rich, not us. And we were going to tell you when you came home. Except you didn't. Until now.'

'Would you have come home sooner if I had told you?' Jessie asked, giving Severine a strange look.

'Of course I would.'

'Why?'

It was a simple question but Severine hesitated.

'Well?' Jessie persisted.

Severine shook her head. 'Because ... because having money makes a difference. It makes everything different.'

'Does it?' Jessie squinted at her. 'I'll accept it has certainly made life easier. There's far less to worry about – like how we were going to pay the bills and how we were going to keep this inn open. But why would it make a difference as far as you visiting your family is concerned? Are you saying you didn't come home because you couldn't afford the ticket? Didn't you have a return ticket when you left?'

'Yes of course I had a return ticket. And anyway, Harvey's rich, remember? He would've paid for a flight.'

'Then why?'

Molly squeezed Severine's hand again. 'Yes, darling. Why?'

Severine shook her head and stared at her plate. 'I don't know why. It just does.'

She was telling the truth. She had no idea why her family acquiring such sudden wealth would have made any difference to her plans. Or why she would've come home sooner if she had known. But something deep inside her was telling her it would have made a difference.

It did make a difference.

It does.

Chapter Thirteen

Severine sat in the lounge, drinking a mug of hot chocolate and peering out the window at the view across the choppy waters between Snowflake Isle and the town of Michaelmas Bay. She had loved this view as a child. She had loved Snowflake Cove in those days. Loved her family and friends. Loved the simple things in life.

When had that all changed?

She still loved her family, but not in the way she had when she was young. And Snowflake Inn would always have a place in a heart, even if that place had grown smaller over the years.

Why couldn't she just be like Evie? Happy and bubbly, come what may. Satisfied with her lot in life. Although now that Evie had Zachary Thorn as a boyfriend, Evie's lot in life looked a whole lot brighter than it had. But Severine had never been like that. She had always wanted more. Always felt there was something missing. She hated being poor. Although by most people's standards the Starr family had never been that. Until the last couple of years. But as Severine had been living in London for the past fifteen years, that hadn't really affected her. She had felt poor, though, growing up. She had seen all the wealthy holidaymakers driving down to Snowflake Cove in their fancy cars. Her schoolfriends had spent their summer holidays abroad. Severine had spent hers on the beaches of Snowflake Isle.

'Why would you want to go anywhere else?' Jessie had asked her on one occasion when Severine had watched a plane high above on its way to far off climes. 'People dream of living in a place like this. You don't know how lucky you are, little one.'

'We're poor,' Severine had said, sulkily kicking at a sandcastle her sister, Evie and their friend, Logan Dorset, who seemed to spend every summer holiday with them, had built.

'We're rich,' Jessie had replied. 'Rich beyond compare. Maybe not in money but we're rich in love and family. And nothing on earth can compare with that.'

The rest of the Starrs may have felt rich in love and family but somehow Severine hadn't. Although she had spent most of her life trying to be.

'Mum!'

'Raven!' Severine turned around the second she heard her daughter's voice.

Raven ran towards her. 'When did you get here?'

'Hours ago.' Severine swept her up in a hug. A hug that surprised both of them in its intensity.

'You should've texted me to say you were here.'

'I texted to say I was coming.'

Raven nodded against Severine's shoulder. 'But I'd arranged to go out with Dad. I couldn't cancel.'

'No, of course not. Why stay here and wait for your mum who's been with you all your life when you can go out with a man who abandoned you before you were born and only turned up a few weeks ago.'

Raven pushed away from Severine and fixed her with a tearful glare.

'That's not fair, Mum! And it's not very nice. And you haven't been here for the last two months. You've been in New York. Then Las Vegas, planning to get married to a man I hardly know, and without *me* at your wedding! Then back in New York. You could've come home long before now. But you didn't. I almost died, but you still didn't come home. Dad did. He saw that news report and he got on the first plane he could. You didn't.'

'Don't speak to me like that. I'm your mother.'

'Then act like it.'

'How dare you! And after everything I've done for you. All the things I've given up. Do you begrudge me just a little bit of happiness?'

'Of course not. I want you to be happy. We all do. But you're my mum. You should've been here. You should've come home. You shouldn't have left me.'

'I didn't leave you. And if you'd come with me and Harvey, none of this would've happened. You were the one who didn't want to go to New York. I asked you to come and you wouldn't.'

'No, you didn't!' Raven's voice reached fever pitch. 'What you actually said was that you were going to New York with Harvey, to meet his family, and that you knew I wouldn't want to go because I don't like big cities and I'd rather spend time with my aunt and my grandparents. You didn't ask me if I wanted to go.'

'I did! Of course I did. Didn't I? I'm sure I did. But anyway, it was true.'

'Really? It may have escaped your notice, Mum, but we live in London. That's a pretty big city.'

'We … We live on the outskirts. Not in the city. New York's not like that.'

'Yeah, right.'

Was that actually the way it had happened? Had she made a decision for her daughter without even asking Raven what she wanted to do?

'Please don't be cross with me, darling. I really can't take it. I've had about as much aggro as I can stand today. Especially in my condition.' She rubbed her hand in a circular motion over her lightly swollen tummy.

Raven looked contrite. 'Are you … Are you OK?'

Severine sat on the nearest chair and smiled wanly. 'I'm fine. Just tired. And a little anxious.'

Raven sat beside her. 'About the baby? Is something wrong?'

'No.' Severine shook her head and took her daughter's hand in hers. 'The baby is fine. As far as I know. I'm anxious about you. About you and me. You do know I love you, don't you? That you're the most important person in the world to me?'

Raven looked a bit doubtful but she nodded. 'I know you love me. And I love you, Mum. I really do. It's just that sometimes …' Her voice trailed off.

'Sometimes?'

Raven met her eyes. 'Don't get mad.'

'I won't get mad.'

'Well … I do love you. But sometimes … I don't like you very much. And not just you. Sometimes I don't like myself very much either. We're moody, Mum. And we sulk if we don't get our own way. And … and we're selfish.'

'Nonsense. Who the hell has told you that? Was it Roggero? Did he say that?'

'No Mum.'

'Jessie? It was Jessie, wasn't it? She always has preferred Evie to me.'

'No, Mum. It wasn't Dad and it wasn't Grammy. I'm saying it. And I'm saying it because it's true. But I'm getting better … Nicer. At least I hope I am. You can be nicer too. You've just got to try.'

'I've got to what?'

'You said you wouldn't get mad.'

'But I …' Severine saw the expression on Raven's face and let out a long, sorrowful sigh. 'Is that really what you think? That I could be nicer?'

Raven nodded and shrugged. 'But I guess everyone could be nicer, couldn't they? I just think … Well … I just think you and I need to try a bit harder than other people. That's all.'

Severine held her daughter's gaze for several seconds before pulling Raven into her arms and hugging her tight. She kissed the top of Raven's head; brushed her long black hair with one hand and then whispered in her ear. 'When did you get to be so smart? I'm supposed to be the adult here. I think you're telling me I've got a lot to learn.'

Raven eased herself away and smiled, her eyes filling with tears which she swiped away with one hand. 'We've both got a lot to learn, Mum. Can we do that together?'

'Of course we can, darling. Of course.'

'And you won't get cross when I want to see Dad?'

Severine frowned. 'I'll try not to.'

'And … and what about moving to New York? Do I … do I really have to go?'

Severine squeezed Raven's hands. 'Do you honestly not want to? Do you hate the thought that much?'

'I want to be with you. So if you want to live in New York, then I suppose …' Raven shrugged. 'But I'd like to spend lots of time here, too. With Grammy, Granny M and everyone. And … and with Dad.' She glanced at her mum beneath her lashes.

Severine took a deep breath. She really didn't want to have this conversation now.

'Well let's see, shall we? We don't have to make any decisions today. And from what I hear, we've got a party to go to tonight. Have you got something lovely to wear?'

Raven's excitement shone in her dark eyes, all animosity and anxiety temporarily forgotten. Eyes so much like her father's that just looking into them made something in Severine's heart do a little flip.

'Dad bought me a dress. I wanted a really sexy red one but everyone said it made me look like a tart. So I got the pink one instead.'

'Pink? But you hate pink.'

'Not any more. It's a dark pink. Cerise or something, Dad called it. He said it brings out the colour of my eyes and hair.'

Severine could almost hear him saying that. 'Oh, did he?'

Raven turned and grabbed one of the bags she had dropped on the floor when she first came in.

'I'll show you.' She pulled out a dress from reams of tissue paper and shook it, standing up and holding it against her. 'It's a very girly dress and I wasn't sure about it at first, but everyone said they liked it, so … Do you like it, Mum?'

It was certainly a beautiful dress. Definitely cerise; it had gossamer, three-quarter length sleeves, a sweetheart neckline, and a slightly lighter pink velvet belt around the waist, which tied at the front and from which a stream of ribbons, in every shade of pink, cascaded down to the hem a few inches above Raven's knees.

'Like it?' Severine said, a catch in her throat. 'I love it. You and Rog … your father have excellent taste.'

Damn the man.

Chapter Fourteen

Luna, Jane and Mason arrived at Logan's restaurant thirty minutes early. Jane had said she wanted to be certain they had plenty of time and was also a little anxious in case Logan needed any help. As the minicab pulled up outside, Luna couldn't believe her eyes.

'Is this it?'

'Yes dear,' Jane replied, tapping Luna on her knee as if she were trying to calm an excited child.

Luna beamed at Mason. 'It's called Moonlight!'

'So it is, sweetheart. So it is. Er. I'm afraid I shall need your assistance.'

'Oh yes. Sorry.'

Luna stepped on to the pavement and helped Jane get out before going to the front passenger side to help her uncle.

'I'll do it, love.' The driver appeared, holding Mason's crutches which he'd previously placed in the boot, and Luna moved out of the way.

Jane had an odd expression on her face.

'Are you OK?' Luna asked.

'You seemed surprised by the name,' Jane said.

Luna smiled. 'It's called Moonlight.'

'I know it is, dear.'

'Moonlight is my passion. That's what I photograph. What I paint. Virtually everything I do involves moonlight. Isn't that a huge coincidence?' She struggled to contain her excitement.

'Yes it is, dear. Well I never. Would you like to know why it's called Moonlight?'

Luna nodded as Mason thanked the cab driver and eased himself towards her with a clickety-clack of his crutches on the cobbled pavement.

'It's because Logan's dad – my only son – was always saying that he would buy a boat when he retired and that he and his family would sail it around the world. He was going to call it Moonlight. Logan thought it would be a fitting tribute. It's not a boat, but it does overlook the marina, and the boats anchored there.' She bobbed her head towards the water just a few feet away, where the waves were pounding the stone walls of the promenade which were keeping the swirling waves at bay. 'I think it's a wonderful sentiment, don't you?'

'Absolutely.'

Luna could see that talking about this was upsetting Jane and without thinking, she gave her a quick hug.

'Well, Mason.' Jane clearly wanted to change the subject. 'Let's get you inside. The wind is picking up again and if you fall over I'm not sure Luna and I will be able to get you up.'

'I probably shouldn't have come,' Mason said. Not in a self-pitying way, but in a matter-of-fact manner. 'I don't want to be a burden. But you did both insist.'

'Nonsense,' Jane said, marching ahead. 'You won't be a burden. And we knew that you didn't really want to miss this.'

Luna fell into step beside her uncle.

'I wonder if Logan would consider having some of my photographs and paintings on display. It would be such a perfect opportunity for me and it would tie in so brilliantly with the name of the restaurant. You didn't tell me it was called Moonlight.'

'I don't recall it being mentioned. If it had, I would have asked the lad myself about taking your artwork. I think it's an excellent idea. I'll put a word in Jane's ear but I'm sure you can persuade Logan without any help from us. He's a handsome young man, after all, and you're a beautiful young woman.'

Luna remembered the last time she and a handsome young man had discussed artwork. Her mother's sculptures. And that hadn't worked out so well. Perhaps she had better find another outlet for her pictures. The last thing she needed in her life right now was a man and complications. Although – unless she was completely on the wrong track – she was pretty sure that Logan's interests lay elsewhere. If the way he had looked at Severine Starr and defended her against his gran was anything to go by, Logan Dorset was very much in love with someone else. Luna stood very little chance of getting his attention, let alone of him being attracted to her.

Not that she wanted that.

Did she?

No. This was strictly business. If Logan was willing to display her artwork, she would happily give him a percentage of the profits.

'Thanks, Mason. Let's see what the situation is once we get inside. He may already have his walls plastered in art. If that's the case, I'd rather not put him on the spot and make him feel under any obligation to help a friend of his gran's.'

'Come along, you two,' Jane said. 'There's a drink in here with my name on it. And I mean that literally. Logan has a friend who makes cocktails in one of those posh hotels in London. He's invented a cocktail for Logan, called The Moonlight and another called Jane's Undoing, just for me.' Jane giggled like a twenty-year-old at a hen night.

'I like the sound of that,' Mason said. Then leaning closer to Luna he added, 'I was rather hoping I would be Jane's undoing, but at my age and in this condition, I'll take all the help I can get.' He winked, and the clickety-clack of his crutches clicked and clacked much faster.

Luna smiled and followed Jane and Mason into the restaurant.

Logan spotted them the second the door opened.

'Hello, Gran. You're looking lovely as always.'

'So are you. I'm so proud of you, Logan. Is your mother here? She called to say she would come straight here because she was running late.'

Logan nodded. 'She arrived a few minutes ago. She's in the room upstairs, getting changed. Hello, Mason. I'm so glad you made it. I didn't think you would. Here. Let me take your coats. Come and sit down before it gets too crowded and we're playing musical chairs with the seats.'

He smiled at Luna and she saw him look her up and down as she removed her coat.

'You came,' he said. 'You look stunning.'

She handed him her coat. 'Thanks. You look pretty good yourself. I love the name of your restaurant.'

'Thanks. It has special significance to me.'

'Yes. Your gran told me about your dad. I'm so sorry. But I think what you've done is a testament to your love for him. He'd be exceedingly proud, I'm sure.'

Logan gave her a wistful smile. 'Thank you. That means a lot.' Then he grinned mischievously.

'Of course, that depends on whether or not anyone gets food poisoning from the oysters. He might not be so proud if they do. Let me get you all some drinks.'

He handed the coats to a girl dressed in a pale silver-grey skirt and blouse.

'She looks like a moonbeam,' Luna said.

Logan raised his brows. 'Phew. That's what we were going for. Mum suggested it. I wanted something different from the traditional black and white. It seemed like a good idea in my head but I was worried it wouldn't work out in reality. I was concerned the staff would look as if we'd wrapped them in tin foil ready for the oven.'

Luna smiled. 'You're fine. Tin foil didn't even enter my head. Although now you mention it … Don't worry. I'm joking.'

Jane and Mason sat at a table near the bar and Luna joined them as Logan got the attention of one of the waiters.

'Champagne, Gran?' Logan asked. 'Or would you like your cocktail?'

'Cocktail first. Champagne later.' She beamed. 'I feel like the Queen. Having a drink named after me. I know she has ships and things, but a cocktail is more up my street.'

Logan smiled. 'Luna? With your name, you've got to try the house cocktail. It's called The Moonlight.'

'Yes please. This place looks perfect, Logan. Congratulations.'

'It does, sweetheart,' Jane added.

'And it's so different from what was here before,' Mason said. 'This looks very up-market.'

Logan looked pleased. 'I'm glad you think so. I wish I'd ordered some artwork for the walls. I meant to, but I couldn't find what I was looking for and then time got away from me. Actually, the truth is, I forgot. I was going to dash out and buy something this morning but I got a bit side-tracked and then it went out of my head.'

The waiter brought the drinks and the second he handed Luna hers, she took two large gulps.

'What's wrong?' Logan was saying, darting looks between Mason and Luna. 'You're both giving me very odd looks. Have I got spinach in my teeth or something? Or are you simply thinking what an absolute berk I am for forgetting something like that?'

Luna's cheeks flushed as all eyes turned to her. 'Gosh. That's delicious. Um. Sorry. No. You're not a berk and your teeth are perfect. I mean … Um … It's just that… Um …'

Mason came to her rescue. 'It just so happens that Luna is an artist and photographer. And, by a rather strange quirk of fate, her artwork is predominately pictures of the moonlight in all its various glories.'

'Oh. I'd forgotten that,' said Jane.

Logan was clearly astonished. 'You're kidding. Seriously? That's incredible. Do you have any with you?'

For some absurd reason, Luna glanced at her clutch bag. 'Not here. And most of it's in transit. On its way from Spain. But it should be here within the next couple of days. Not that that helps you now.'

'You could borrow some of the pictures Luna has sent me over the years,' Mason suggested. 'But I'd want them back, of course. I'm sure she wouldn't mind popping back to the cottage and grabbing a few, if you'd like. Although banging nails into the walls just before your guests arrive might not be such a good idea.'

'It's a great idea,' Logan said. 'Oh. But Luna may not—'

'I'd be happy to.' Luna jumped to her feet. 'I'll go right now. It'll only take about fifteen minutes if I get the cab to wait.'

'I'll come with you,' Logan said.

Jane looked horrified. 'On your opening night?'

Logan's mum appeared from the doorway to one side of the kitchen, leading upstairs.

'Hello Jane. What's going on?'

'Mum!' Logan beamed. 'This is perfect. You can hold the fort. Luna is an artist. We're dashing to Mason's to get some of her pictures for the walls. We'll call a cab.'

Not in the least bit perplexed, his mum smiled. 'Take my car. It'll be quicker. You've got plenty of time. Guests won't start arriving until seven at the earliest and it's only just gone six-thirty now.'

Logan kissed her on the cheek. 'Thanks, Mum. You're the best.'

She grinned. 'I know. And you can introduce me to this lovely young lady when you get back.'

'Oh sorry! I wasn't thinking. Mum, this is Luna. Luna, this is Mum. Let's go.'

Luna smiled and waved at Logan's mum as he dashed towards the back door which Luna assumed would lead to a car park. 'It's lovely to meet you.' She followed him and stepped outside as he held the door open.

'And you, dear. We'll talk more later.'

'You're a lifesaver,' Logan said, opening the car door for Luna.

'Actually, you're doing me a huge favour.'

Logan got in and a second later they were heading towards Bell Cottage.

'Oh? How's that? I'm the one who needs the artwork.'

She took a deep breath. 'Yes. But I'm the one who needs to earn a living and was going to be really cheeky and ask if you'd be interested in a proposition.'

He shot her a look and grinned. 'A proposition? That sounds intriguing.'

'Don't get too excited.'

'Are you cold? You're shivering. Sorry, I should've grabbed your coat.'

'I wasn't shivering. I…' She couldn't tell him that several rather naughty thoughts popped into her head because of the way he'd looked at her.

'I'm fine. Anyway, what I was going to propose is that you could hang a few of my pictures and possibly offer them for sale, or alternatively, display a few of my business cards. I'd give you a percentage of any money I make from sales, or a flat fee if it was just the cards.'

'Wow! This must be fate. I need pictures. You need somewhere to display yours. It's perfect. As for a percentage, let's just agree that you keep my walls covered for free and I'll display your art for free. Deal?'

'Are you sure? I seem to be getting the best of the bargain. And you haven't seen my pictures yet. You might hate them.'

'I'm sure. And I don't think I'll hate them. Unless they're some sort of abstract art. I'm not a huge fan of that. They're not, are they? I think I've seen some of the pictures hanging on Mason's walls and if they were yours, I like them already.'

Luna smiled. 'I'm not a fan of abstract art either. Mine are simply photographs and paintings of the moon and moonlight, over land and sea, some using a variety of mediums and filters.'

'Great. So do we have a deal?'

She smiled. 'We have a deal. But if you hate them, I'll give you a chance to back out.'

'I won't back out.'

Seconds later, they pulled up outside Bell Cottage.

'We're here.'

'Don't sound so surprised, Luna. It's not that far and I was probably exceeding the speed limit.'

They got out and dashed into the cottage and Luna pointed out the first painting hanging in the hall. It was a black and white photo of the moon over the hills behind her parents' house in Spain. The house she had just sold.

'I love that,' Logan said. 'May I borrow it?'

Luna nodded. A momentary rush of sadness and longing for the past, swept over her but she quickly regained her composure and moved on. Within a matter of minutes, both of them had their arms full of photographs and paintings.

'I should've brought a box to put them in,' Logan said, as they headed back to the car.

'Do you have a hammer and nails at the restaurant?' Luna asked.

He threw her a doubtful look. 'I'm not sure.'

'Wait there one minute. I'll grab Mason's toolbox from under the stairs.'

She raced back into the cottage and when she came out, Logan was staring across the channel separating the mainland from Snowflake Isle, his eyes firmly fixed on the doorway to Snowflake Inn. He seemed oblivious of her return.

'Logan? Logan? We can go.'

He turned his head to look at her and there was sadness in his eyes. And something more. Something akin to … longing.

'Sorry,' he said, far less exuberant than he had been. 'I was miles away.'

Luna had an unpleasant feeling that she knew exactly where his thoughts had taken him. And for some unfathomable reason, it bothered her far more than it should.

Chapter Fifteen

Minicabs, to ferry everyone to Logan's restaurant were waiting in the car park of Snowflake Cove, a few minutes before seven. Due to the number of people going, there were several cabs, and they jostled for space amongst the residents' cars.

Severine, who had astonishingly been the first person to be ready, stood in the doorway of Snowflake Inn watching the drivers negotiate their vehicles in and out of the small opening to the car park. How any of them would cope in a city with real traffic problems, she had no idea. Sipping her glass of Molly's homemade lemonade – and wishing it were wine – she pictured the streets of New York, where car horns blared every couple of seconds and the air frequently turned blue with expletives yelled through hastily opened car windows.

'Hello Severine.'

Severine froze on the spot, even though her heart was racing and her body felt as if it had spontaneously combusted at the sound of that voice. A voice she hadn't heard for more than fifteen years but one she recognised immediately.

She swallowed whatever had caught in her throat and steeled her heart and mind and body to turn around and face Roggero Tazzeone.

'Hello.' Her mouth felt dry so she licked her lips. 'That's it? That's all you have to say to me after all these years?'

Roggero, still as handsome as the last day she had seen him, shrugged and gave a strange little smile.

'It is a start.' He walked towards her, one hand tucked into a pocket of his black trousers, the other fiddling with his tie as if it were a fraction too tight. 'You have not changed at all.'

'So everyone keeps telling me.'

She had forgotten how tall and svelte he was. Forgotten how his black hair gleamed as if sprayed with metallic paint. Forgotten how his dark eyes could seem so bright and warm and sensual. She must keep her cool. Part of her wanted to run away from him, part wanted to slap his face and another part – a small part – wanted to run into his arms and hold him so tight that he would never be able to walk away from her again.

'You are still very beautiful, Severine.'

Hell's Bells, even her name sounded sexy when he said it.

'And you are still a liar.'

He halted. 'A liar? I do not think I ever lied to you.'

'You said you loved me.'

'I did love you.'

'You said you were going to leave Sylvie.'

'I did leave Sylvie.'

'But not for me! You left me too. I thought we were going to be together forever. I thought you were going to marry me. I thought …'

She sucked in a breath. What was she doing? She gulped her lemonade and looked away. Too many years had passed to be having this conversation now.

'I am sorry, Severine.' He came and stood beside her. 'I was foolish. I was out of my depth. I behaved appallingly to many people. But I do not think I lied. I did not say we would be together. I did not say we would marry. It is not an excuse and I know I must ask for your forgiveness, but I did not lie to you.'

'You just abandoned me. You abandoned our daughter.'

He looked as if he had been punched in the stomach. He closed his eyes for a split second and let out a sigh.

'And that I regret. I regret leaving without telling anyone. I regret running away from my family. From my responsibilities. From you. And from Raven. I regret many things. But I cannot regret loving you. I cannot regret Raven. She is beautiful, Severine. She is a wonderful girl and I thank you with all my heart for having her. For bringing her up and making her the girl that she is. You should be proud. Very proud.'

Severine scanned his face. 'I am proud. As proud as a mother can be. But … I think I owe a lot of what and who she is, to my family. And to my friends in London who helped me. Who babysat whilst I went out to work.' She shook her head. 'You have no idea what it was like for me. For us. And now you come back and want to be the father you never were. How exactly does that work, Roggero?'

He didn't get a chance to answer. Raven hurried towards them, smiling from ear to ear.

'That's a sight I never thought I'd see,' she said. 'My mum and my dad standing in the doorway of my grandparents' inn, chatting away as if we've always been a family.'

Severine and Roggero exchanged glances.

'Neither did I,' Severine whispered, just loud enough for Roggero's ears.

'You will be the most beautiful girl at the party tonight,' Roggero said to Raven, oozing fatherly pride. He gave Severine a sideways look and she only just caught what he said because his voice was so soft and quiet. 'And you, Severine, will be the most beautiful woman.'

'Severine.' Evie was walking towards her hand in hand with Zachary Thorn, whom Severine recognised immediately. 'I'd like you to meet

Zachary. Zachary, this is my older sister, Severine. Raven's mum.'

No wonder Evie had fallen for him. Zachary Thorn was more gorgeous in real life than he looked on TV. And that took some beating.

'Pleased to meet you, Severine,' he was saying, reaching out his free hand. 'I've heard a lot about you.'

'I bet.' Severine took his hand and shook it and was surprised when he pulled her into a hug – albeit briefly.

'You look lovely,' Zachary said. 'You must be so glad to be home. I love New York but it's definitely not Snowflake Cove, is it?'

'You can say that again.' She didn't think he meant it in the same way she did though. 'Have you just arrived? I didn't see you earlier.'

'Yeah. Filming schedule clashed. It was a bit of a rush but I wouldn't miss Logan's opening party for the world. I've just come from the restaurant, in fact. I nipped in on the way back here. I expect Evie mentioned we're do a bit of filming there tonight. We're going to include it in one of the upcoming shows. It's always so good to give a new business a bit of a boost. Especially when it's a friend.'

'No. Evie didn't mention it.' She shot a look at Evie. 'Do you know Logan then, Zachary?'

He nodded. 'I met him when my family, my film crew and I all stayed here.'

'At Christmas?'

105

'Yes. It's such a pity you weren't here. It was one of the best Christmases we've ever had.'

'Apart from when Roland and I fell over the cliff,' Raven said, grinning up at him.

Zachary grinned back. 'Oh yeah. Apart from that.'

'But that brought Dad back to me,' Raven added. 'So actually, it was a great Christmas.'

'Ah yes,' Severine said. 'It seems I have a great deal to thank you for, Zachary, and not just saving my daughter's life. For that, I owe you a huge debt of gratitude. I'm not sure I'll ever be able to repay you.' She gave him her sweetest smile.

'No repayment necessary.' He wrapped an arm around Evie and winked at Raven. 'And we've got a party to get to, so we'd better make a move.'

'Don't wait for me, will you!' Jessie said, with a distinct hint of sarcasm as she walked towards them, followed closely by Molly and John.

Evie laughed. 'We are waiting. We wouldn't dream of going anywhere without *you*!' She winked at Jessie. 'Especially now you're the wealthiest woman we know.'

Jessie chuckled. 'You're dating the grandson of a multi-millionaire. And he's pretty well off in his own right. And if I know anything about anything – which I do – it won't be long until the two of you tie the knot. Not that money has ever mattered to you, Evie Starr. Not one jot. Unlike someone else we know.'

Severine saw the look Jessie gave her and was about to respond when Raven linked her arm through Severine's and smiled. Severine bit back the unpleasant retort wavering on the tip of her tongue and instead asked, 'Do you need any assistance, Gran?' She smiled broadly. 'Here, take my arm and lean on me.' She wasn't sure who was the most surprised – Jessie or herself.

Was this what Raven meant by being nicer? If so, this wasn't going to be that hard. And even if it was, it would be worth it just to see the look on Jessie and the rest of her family's faces.

'Don't you think you'd better put that glass down first, darling?' Molly said, beaming at her.

'Oops! Silly me. I was so eager to help, I completely forgot I had it.'

'That's a sentence I never thought I'd hear,' Jessie said, but a faint smile curved her thin lips as she studied Severine's face.

'Let me take it from you,' Roggero said, brushing his hand against Severine's as he did so.

'Why not,' she said, hardly audible even to Roggero. 'You took everything else from me.'

Chapter Sixteen

The opening party of Moonlight was a complete success. Everyone who had been invited, turned up and the restaurant was full to bursting. Residents and friends from Snowflake Cove brushed shoulders and chatted happily with the Mayor and several wealthy and influential businessmen from Michaelmas Bay. All the guests were having a good time. Delicious food was plentiful and the drink was flowing like a river. The cocktails seemed to be going down a treat, especially The Moonlight. And towards the end of the evening, when one of the guests pointed out that the real moon was almost full tonight, it seemed a prime opportunity for everyone to gather outside as Zachary and his crew filmed several shots of the restaurant and the party-goers bathed in the silvery glow of the moon.

'Did you plan to open tonight because of the moon?' Luna asked, when Logan came up, squeezed her arm and asked if she was enjoying herself.

He pulled a face. 'You won't believe this, but it didn't even occur to me to check.' He glanced up at the moon hanging low over the hills like a perfectly round, massive opal. 'I couldn't have planned it better though, could I? And bearing in mind that earlier tonight there was nothing but cloud, the fact that they've disappeared, leaving a sky full of stars – and that moon – is almost a miracle.'

'Or a sign from your dad to show how pleased and proud he is.'

Their eyes met and something in Logan's made Luna feel as if she were bathed in scorching hot sunlight, not the cool silver-white of the moon. The wind had dropped and the waves now lapped gently against the stone walls a short distance from where they stood. She could see that the waters beyond glistened as moonbeams danced on rippling waves and the boats bobbed in the marina. Logan had his back to the sea and his gaze was firmly fixed on her.

'You're shivering,' he said, his voice soft and oh so sexy.

'I'm not shivering.' She looked deep into his eyes.

'I think I've had a bit too much to drink.' He held his empty glass a fraction in the air but his gaze remained glued on her.

'Me too. I'm not sure where my glass is though.'

'Loads of people have commented on your pictures. They're going down a storm. Your phone will be ringing non-stop.'

Luna nodded. 'I've had lots of compliments. I'm so pleased, Logan. And truly grateful. I don't know how I can ever repay you for this chance.'

'There's nothing to repay. I told you. I'm indebted to you.'

She shook her head and smiled. 'I'm thrilled I was able to help. Your restaurant is going to be a great success, Logan. I can feel it.'

'We make a good team. I think we may both have a bright future ahead of us.'

'I hope so.'

'Luna?' He moved a fraction closer.

'Yes, Logan.'

'Is something …? Are you feeling …?'

'There you are, Logan!' Severine shattered the moment. 'I thought you'd gone back inside. I wanted to congratulate you. I didn't get a chance earlier.' She spotted Luna. 'Oh, hello. We met on the train, didn't we?' She didn't give Luna time to reply. She wrapped her arms around Logan and kissed him full on the mouth.

To Luna's utmost horror, Logan returned Severine's embrace and even worse than that, he returned her kiss with what could only be described as unbridled passion. Luna quickly closed her gaping mouth and ran back into the restaurant as fast as she could without catching her stiletto sandals on the cobbles and falling flat on her face.

Although she felt as if that was exactly what she had done.

Chapter Seventeen

Severine knew she shouldn't have kissed Logan even before she did so, but Roggero had been sending furtive glances in her direction all evening and it was making her feel uneasy. The man was too damn handsome for his own good and no matter how much she turned her thoughts to Harvey and New York, all she kept seeing was Roggero and that damn beach on Snowflake Isle. She had to put a stop to this nonsense now. And what better way to do that than to kiss Logan Dorset?

What she hadn't expected – not even for one second – was for Logan to kiss her back.

She closed her eyes to try to blot out the memory but it didn't work. Her skin still tingled, her heart still pounded and her insides turned to goo every time she thought about it. And she had thought about it a lot since leaving the party and getting into bed.

It must be her hormones. They went haywire when you were expecting.

Oh. My. God!

What was she doing? What was she thinking? She was pregnant and about to marry Harvey and yet here she was thinking about bloody Logan Dorset! Of all people. How the hell did that happen?

And she'd only kissed Logan because she wanted to stop thinking about Roggero.

Was she completely mad!

She had to stop it. Stop it now.

She loved Harvey. She was going to marry Harvey. She was moving to New York. She was going to have his baby. How in hell could she give so much as a second thought to Roggero? Or Logan?

Oh Hell's Bells.

Think of Harvey. Picture Harvey. Imagine your life with Harvey. Remember how good sex is with Harvey.

But the minute she closed her eyes she saw Logan's face. Part passion, part fear, part astonishment bubbling in his huge eyes when their lips had finally parted.

When he'd spoken her name, it was as if he was surprised to see her standing in front of him. Surprised and bewildered.

'Severine?' he'd said, his voice hoarse. 'What the …? How did you …? Where is …?'

The man hadn't been able to form a complete and intelligible sentence.

'Wow, Logan,' she had replied. 'I hadn't expected that. If I'd known you were that good a kisser, I'd have done that years ago.'

'I wish you had,' he said, still looking somewhat discombobulated.

And although she hadn't meant to, she had only gone and damn well kissed the man again.

Oh Hell. Oh Hell. Oh Hell!

'Severine,' he had said, clearly struggling with his own demons. 'What's going on?'

She looked into his eyes. 'I have no idea, Logan. I can't even blame alcohol because I haven't had any. Unless someone has spiked the lemonade.'

'I think I've had too much. Not lemonade. Alcohol.' He seemed even more astonished to realise that he was still holding his empty glass and he waved it in front of her. 'Look. Empty.'

'So I see.' She should have taken that moment to ease herself out of their embrace, but she didn't want to. 'You never knew this, Logan, but I used to have one hell of a crush on you.'

He held her at arm's length and frowned. 'No, you didn't. You never had any interest in me. It was the other way around.'

'I did, Logan. For a long time, in fact. But you always seemed more interested in Evie than me. And then ... well, you know all about Roggero.'

'Roggero! Yep. I know all about him. Did you … did you really have a crush on me? You're not just saying this because … because you think it's what I want to hear?'

'I had the biggest crush ever. In fact, I think I may still have a bit of one now.'

He stared at her as if he was experiencing difficulty with his focus. 'I've been in love with you all my life, Severine. All. My. Life. Since the first time I saw you on the beach and you smiled at me. I fell in love hook, line and sinker, and I've never managed to stop, even when you were being an absolute cow. Even when you fell in love with Roggero. Even now, when you're in love with someone else and going to have his baby and move thousands of miles away, I'm still in love with you. Dumb, huh?'

'Is that true?' She couldn't believe what he had told her. 'You've … you've loved me all your life?'

He nodded. 'Uh huh.'

'Why didn't you tell me?'

He shrugged. 'I didn't think you'd want to hear. I was going to but … you fell for Roggero, so I kept it to myself. And then Dad died.'

'Oh Logan,' she had said. And fell into his arms yet again.

God alone knows what would have happened if her mum, Molly hadn't come outside at that precise moment.

Although that had opened up a whole new can of worms and despite the fact that Molly hadn't said a word to Severine at the time, or apparently to anyone else since they left the party, Severine was fairly certain, there would be words. And most of them weren't going to be pleasant, loving, or happy. Severine was pretty sure of that. She couldn't face an inquisition, feeling as she did, so she had taken the opportunity to sneak up to her room before anyone had a chance to notice. Recriminations and lectures could wait until the morning. What she needed was a good night's sleep to help her figure this out.

She pulled the duvet over her head and shut her eyes tight.

How had life suddenly got so crazy?

Chapter Eighteen

Logan opened his eyes and wished to God he hadn't. Sunlight seared his irises and his head exploded like a supernova, or it felt as if it had. His mouth was parched and his brain thumped against whatever was left of his skull. Just how much had he had to drink last night? He couldn't remember a thing.

He tumbled out of bed and reluctantly padded downstairs, his eyes half closed against the light and one hand on his head to stop it falling from his shoulders.

'So you're awake at last.' It was his gran's voice – and she didn't sound happy.

'Nope. Still asleep. Just came down for some paracetamol.'

'You'll be needing more than paracetamol, my boy. A lot, lot more than that.'

He tried to open his eyes fully but failed, so he opened one and closed the other instead.

'Have I done something to upset you, Gran?'

'Upset me? Why should I be upset?'

He fell on to a vacant chair and slumped forward on the table.

'I don't know. But I can tell you are. I've got the hangover from hell and I can't remember a thing about last night. Please, just put me out of this misery and shoot me now.'

'Shoot you? I think it'll be more of a public hanging if word gets out. How could you do it, Logan? How? And on your opening night of all nights.'

He tried again to open his eyes. 'That sounds serious. Just tell me what I've done. Is Mum furious with me too? Where is Mum?'

'She's at Snowflake Inn, trying to sort things out with Molly. I would have gone but it's absolutely pouring and your dear mother wouldn't hear of me going out in this weather.'

'With Molly? Sorry, Gran. I haven't a clue what you're talking about. If I did something wrong, please tell me. And then please tell me where the paracetamol are. I'm dying here. I don't think I've ever been this hungover in my entire life. Strange bells are clanging in my head.'

'That's the rain bouncing off the gutters. Do you honestly not remember?'

He shook his head. Which was a big mistake.

Jane got to her feet, rummaged around in one of the cupboards and produced a strip of pain

118

killers. She filled a glass with water and placed it in Logan's hands.

'Then let me be the one to fill you in.'

She resumed her seat, banging her mug down on the table far more loudly than was necessary to Logan's way of thinking.

'The evening was going so well. You and your restaurant were a complete success. Until for some reason that I can only put down to alcohol poisoning, or complete insanity, you decided that last night would be a good time to, not only passionately kiss Severine Starr but to also pronounce your undying love for the evil little witch!'

Logan's head shot up, his mouth fell open and suddenly, he could open his eyes, wider in fact, than he would have thought possible.

'I … did … what?'

'Which part requires clarification? The kiss? Or the pronouncement? Tell me, have you completely forgotten the fact that the woman is engaged to someone else? Oh, and pregnant. Let's not forget that part.'

'Shit. Sorry. Didn't mean to use that language. But wow. Did I … did I do it in front of everyone?' He cringed at the thought of that.

'Not everyone, no. Thankfully. Just Molly, I believe. And your mother caught the tail end of it. That's why she's gone to see Molly this morning. To find out exactly what happened.'

'I can't believe it. I kissed Severine? Last night? And … and told her I loved her? Wow.' He threw a tablet into his mouth and swallowed it down with a gulp of water.

'That's it? Wow? That's all you've got to say for yourself? I strongly suggest you take the rest of those tablets, my boy.'

An odd little grin crept across his lips. 'You'd think, after all these years of wanting to do that, I'd actually remember it when I finally did.' He swallowed a second tablet and another gulp of water before giving a half-hearted laugh.

'It's not in the least bit funny, Logan. How could you do such a thing?'

He grimaced at his gran's obvious distress.

'What's the big deal, Gran? So I made a complete and utter fool of myself. I was drunk. I was caught up in the excitement of last night. It was wrong, yes. It was no doubt embarrassing for everyone concerned, but it's hardly the end of the world. Severine will be off to New York before we know it. As a matter of interest, how did Severine take my no doubt clumsy attempt to win her?' He rubbed his cheek. 'I don't recall being slapped, but then again, I don't recall kissing her and I really should be able to remember that, so…' He shrugged.

'She didn't slap you. And that's half the problem. From what I've been told, the damn woman wanted to know why you'd never told her how you felt before. As if it might have made a difference. Dear God and everything that is holy, Logan, if you start an affair with Severine Starr, you'll be looking for a new roof to do it under.'

'Start an affair ...? What *are* you talking about? Severine's not interested in me. She never has been, unfortunately.'

'Oh really? Well, she was certainly interested last night, or so your mother said. Severine not only returned your kisses with equal ardour, she clung to you as if she had no intention of ever letting you go. And that, believe me, can only spell disaster.'

'Severine kissed me back? You're sure? You're absolutely sure?'

'Good grief, Logan! Don't look so happy about it. That woman is a menace. A home wrecker. A harlot.'

'You're talking about the woman I'm in love with, Gran. A woman I've been in love with all my life.'

'She's engaged, Logan. And expecting another man's child!'

'I know that, Gran. But I love her. I always have. And there's not a lot I can do about that.'

'Oh dear Lord.' Jane shook her head and reached out her hand. 'Throw me those tablets, Logan. My head is fit to burst.'

Oddly enough, that was exactly how Logan's heart felt.

Chapter Nineteen

Severine walked into the kitchen, saw Molly huddled over the kitchen table, deep in conversation with Logan's mum, and made a hasty, silent retreat. She was desperate for coffee, but didn't think the kitchen was the best place to be this morning. There would be coffee in the bar.

There was. But there was also Evie, who spotted her before she could escape.

'Morning, Severine. Well, well, you've been back for less than a day and already you've got Mum in a panic.'

'Don't start, Evie. I'm not in the mood.'

Evie poured her a cup of coffee and tapped the seat beside her with her hand.

'Want to talk about it? I know we don't get on, but I'm your sister and I love you. If you're unhappy and you want to talk, I'm here for you.'

Severine stared at her. 'Where's Zachary?'

'Gone to work. He left before dawn. I stayed the night in his room which is why I didn't come to my room last night. Did you sleep OK?'

Severine sat beside Evie and cradled the cup of coffee.

'I'm not sure I slept at all. How do you do it, Evie? How do you sail through life without any complications? Without making waves? I can't seem to stay out of stormy waters and my life gets more complicated every day.'

Evie looked her in the eye. 'You do seem to get yourself into a bit of a mess every so often. What's happened this time? I know it has something to do with Logan Dorset, but I have no idea what.'

'Where do I start?'

'Try the beginning. That usually works.' Evie gave Severine a friendly nudge.

'I'm not sure where the beginning is. That's half the problem.' She sighed and took a gulp of coffee. 'Did you know I had a crush on Logan when we were younger?'

Evie nodded. 'Yes. And I always thought he had a crush on you.'

'Did you? That's odd, because he was always hanging around you.'

'I think that was because you terrified the life out of him. Actually, you terrified the life out of me, too.'

They glanced at one another and grinned. 'I've always been a bit of a cow, haven't I?'

'You won't get any argument from me on that count. We all loved you though, in spite of that. We still do.'

'You may not, when I tell you my latest, heinous crime.'

'Tell me and we'll see.'

'I kissed Logan, last night. More than once. And I think I told him I had a crush on him. In fact, I know I did.'

'O…K. Why do I get the feeling there's more to come?'

Severine screwed up her face like a Pug dog.

'Logan told me he loved me. That he's always loved me. I mean, *really* loved me. And he said he still does.'

'Bloody hell! Poor Logan.'

'Poor Logan? What about me? I'm in love with Harvey. I'm engaged. I'm expecting our child. So why have I just spent all last night dreaming about bloody, Logan Dorset? Please answer me that. And I'm serious. Why? How can I possibly have done that? I only kissed him because Roggero was looking at me in a way that was seriously making my heart do things it shouldn't. I thought if I kissed Logan, it would get that damn Roggero Tazzeone out of my head. That worked well, didn't it?'

'Whoa!' Evie's coffee cascaded over the rim of her cup. 'You kissed Logan because you were lusting after Roggero? Is that what you're telling me?' She put her cup down with a thud.

'I know. It sounds awful, doesn't it? I've been going over and over it in my head and I simply can't make any sense of it. If I'd been drinking I could understand. But I hadn't. All I had all night was lemonade. Bloody lemonade!'

'Don't get hysterical. Drink your coffee and let's think about this. Who knows? I mean, who saw you? Mum, I assume, because she's been snapping at me all morning and that's not at all like her. She only does that when she's terribly worried about something. And I saw Logan's mum in the kitchen with her, so I think we can safely assume what they're talking about.'

Severine dropped her head into her hands and shook it back and forth.

'Help me, Evie.' She threw her sister a pleading look. 'Please help me.'

'I'm trying to, but I'm honestly not sure I can. Listen. How do you feel about getting Juniper involved? I always go to her for help. Wait. No. That's not a good idea. She may be my best friend but clearly even I'm not thinking straight this morning. We'd have to tell her you were lusting after her dad – again – and I think she's only just forgiven you and him for the last time that happened. OK. I suppose we're on our own. Do you really love him?'

'Logan? Or Roggero?'

Evie smirked. 'I meant your fiancé, Harvey, actually. Do you really love Harvey? I mean, I know you think you do, but do you? Deep down.

Do you love him in the way you loved Roggero all those years ago?'

Severine considered the matter for a few moments.

'Yes. Well, almost. It's not the same. I can't compare Harvey with Roggero.'

'Why not? We could make a list. Write down what you loved about Roggero in one column and what you love about Harvey in another.'

'What about Logan? Should we have a column for him?'

Evie tutted. 'I don't know, Severine. Should we? Only you can answer that. Are you saying that you think you may be a little in love with all three of them? Mum should've sent you to a nunnery when you were young.'

'Don't be horrid. You said you'd help.'

'Sorry. My head is spinning.'

Both Evie and Severine spun round in their seats when they heard a cough behind them.

'That's because you drank too much last night, Evie,' Jessie said. 'Along with several other people, I believe. Not that you have that excuse, Severine.'

Severine shrank into her chair and Evie fidgeted in hers.

'It seems you're making your mark, as usual, miss,' Jessie continued. 'And it also seems you need some advice. Pour me some coffee, Evie.'

Evie did as Jessie asked and handed her the coffee.

Severine took a deep breath. 'If you're going to lecture me, I'd rather not stay here.'

'I am, and you shall. It's about time someone sat you down and sorted you out, Severine Starr. You're like an out of control comet, smashing yourself against anyone and anything you come into contact with whilst headed on a course of ultimate destruction.'

'Thanks, Gran. That's helpful.'

'Don't be sarcastic. If I understand things correctly, you still harbour feelings for Roggero. That's understandable. You need closure. You loved him and he disappeared from your life. Now he's back and is going to be a part of your future whether you like it or not. You have a child together. There will always be that bond. Logan reminds you of happier times. Times when you were carefree and life was teeming with possibilities. You had no responsibilities. No ties. Seeing him again reminded you of a life you could have had. As for Harvey. You've been bringing up a daughter and working full time. Life has been a struggle. You love Raven and she loves you but you've been craving something else. You want to love a man and be loved. In walks Harvey. He fits the bill. You think you're in love. A world of possibilities opens up before you. You can start a new life in New York. You'll never have to work again unless you want to. You'll never have to worry about money. But Raven's not so keen. There's a spanner in the works. So you come home to persuade her and suddenly you're back where you began. Roggero's here. Logan's here. Harvey isn't. That's your problem.'

Severine waited for Jessie to continue but she didn't.

'And?' Evie said, voicing what Severine was thinking.

'Well surely it's clear.' Jessie drank her coffee and smiled. 'If you really love someone. And I mean enough to build a life with them, you don't stop loving them the minute they're not around. You don't suddenly long for your former lover, or the love that got away. You may think about what you no longer have, but you certainly don't have a burning desire to make your former lover jealous, or to kiss someone you had a crush on, to do that. And you certainly don't spend the night tossing and turning and wondering. Yes, I heard everything you said. I was on my way to the lounge but I stopped and listened instead. For heaven's sake, Severine, you only left Harvey's side the day before yesterday. Doesn't that tell you anything? Doesn't that give you a hint?'

Severine and Evie exchanged glances and Severine shook her head.

'Oh, what is the matter with you two? It's as plain as the nose on your face, Severine. You're not in love with Harvey. Not enough to build a life with him. That's very sad. It's incredibly awkward. It's definitely going to be a problem. But it's a fact. There's no getting around it. That's why you

128

were in such a rush to marry the man. You wanted to get it signed and sealed before you changed your mind.'

'That's not true! I love Harvey. I do. I really, really do.'

Jessie shrugged. 'Unfortunately, Severine, saying it won't make it so. You can tell yourself that until you're blue in the face. But you'd be lying. And it won't change a thing. You care about him, I'm sure you do. But love? True love? The sort of love that lasts a lifetime. No. And the sooner you accept that, the sooner you can decide who exactly you do love enough to try to build a life with. And I don't think it takes a genius to work that one out. Now I'm going to tell Molly that I'll die of starvation if she doesn't stop gossiping with Logan's mum and get some breakfast on the table. You sit and think about what I've said. I'm sure you'll be able to work it out in the end.'

'I think I'm more confused now than I was before,' Evie said.

'Imagine how I feel,' said Severine.

Jessie walked towards the door. 'Oh. I'll say one more thing. And this is a clue, Severine, so listen carefully. Before you can love someone else – completely, selflessly, whole-heartedly love someone else, you have got to love yourself.'

Evie gave a hollow laugh. 'Severine definitely loves herself. No offence, Severine.'

Severine threw Evie a look. 'None taken.'

Jessie peered at them.

'Does she? Does she honestly? Only you can answer that one, Severine.'

Chapter Twenty

Luna put a pot of coffee on the kitchen table, a jug of milk, two plates, cutlery and rack of toast before taking a seat opposite her uncle.

'Is everything all right?' Mason asked. 'You seem a little distracted this morning. Do you have a hangover?'

Luna nodded and rubbed her forehead with her hand. 'A slight one.'

'And that's all?'

She met Mason's look. 'Of course. Although I'm probably a little tired, too.'

'Is that why you have forgotten the mugs? Or is there something else troubling you?'

Luna got up and the feet of her chair scraped against the tiled floor. She took two mugs from the shelf and filled them with coffee.

'Nothing's troubling me. I couldn't be happier. I'm here with you. My work is hanging in the newest, trendiest restaurant in Michaelmas Bay and I already have several orders. All my belongings, together with Mum's sculptures and Dad's paintings should be arriving any day now from Spain. I've made new friends and contacts in just one day. The only downside is this weather. I can't remember the last time I've seen rain like this. Oh. I forgot the butter.'

She stood up again and got the butter from the fridge.

'And marmalade, please.'

'Right. Marmalade.'

Mason squeezed her hand when she sat down for the third time.

'I'm aware we haven't seen much of one another over the years, and that's entirely my fault. Perhaps, because of that, I don't know you as well as I think I do, but one thing I do know is that you are just like your mother. Like you, Jasmine was a hopeless liar. She couldn't hide the truth if her life depended on it. Something's wrong, Luna. I know it is. If you don't feel able to tell me, that's fine. Perhaps Jane could help. Or maybe Evie. Or Juniper. She and her boyfriend Darren only live a couple of doors away. And of course Evie is just over the bridge. Jane's next door. If you won't tell me, please tell one of them.'

'Jane's the last person I could tell. And Evie and Juniper are friends with him so …'

She blushed and glanced at Mason.

'Him? Did you say, Him? Is this about Mateus? Are you still upset about that scoundrel? No. It can't be him. Evie and Juniper don't know him.'

She shook her head. 'This has nothing to do with Mateus. Although, perhaps in a way it does.'

'Who then? Ah. I believe the proverbial penny may have dropped. Is this, by any chance, connected to a certain young man who lives next door with his grandmother? A certain young man who seemed to like you, and, if I'm any judge of such things, a man you liked at your first meeting?'

Luna pushed her plate away with the slice of toast she had buttered sitting discarded in the centre.

'I thought he liked me. I was wrong. But that's fine. I don't want to get involved with a man at this stage in my life, anyway. No matter how perfect he seems. And of course, no man's perfect. Logan's no exception. Why should he be?'

'Did something happen?'

'Yes. No. Nearly. Then Severine showed up. I can't believe that woman. I thought she was engaged. And she's definitely pregnant, although it's hardly visible at this stage. But even so, to do what she did is unforgivable, isn't it?'

'I would need to know what it is she did before I can answer that.'

Luna pulled her plate back towards her, grabbed her knife, and slathered marmalade on her toast.

'She kissed Logan Dorset. That's what she did. Full on the lips. Not just a peck on the cheek. A full, and from where I was standing, pretty passionate mouth on mouth kiss.'

Mason looked horrified. 'She did what? Good heavens! What was the woman thinking?'

Luna let out a derisive laugh. 'I believe I can tell you precisely what she was thinking.'

'And Logan? What did Logan do?'

'He kissed her right back. Passionately, wantonly, desperately. And I definitely know what he was thinking.'

'Good gracious. Well, that is certainly a surprise. What happened then?'

'Your guess is as good as mine. I left them to it.' Luna bit into her toast and pulled a face. 'This has got marmalade on.' She tossed it back on to her plate. 'I don't like marmalade.'

Mason sighed, took the toast and ate it himself.

'I think what you need today, is a complete distraction. What can we do in this torrential rain?'

A vision popped into Luna's head, but it didn't involve Mason. It involved a boat in Michaelmas Bay, with rain bouncing on the polished wood of the deck, on which two people were standing, their arms wrapped around one another in a passionate embrace and their drenched clothes clinging to their damp skin. One of those people was Luna, the other, a certain restaurateur, who unfortunately was madly in love with someone else.

Chapter Twenty-One

Gossip usually spread like wildfire in the tiny village of Snowflake Cove, so Severine was expecting the worst. She wanted to get away from it if possible for a few hours at least. She and Evie decided to go out after their conversation with Jessie. Severine needed some time to figure things out, but she had never been a fan of doing things alone, and had asked her sister to go with her. On a day like today, with torrential rain, walking on the beach of Snowflake Isle was about as much fun as jumping in a bath of iced water. Neither Evie nor Severine found that prospect appealing. Instead, they were going to catch a bus into Michaelmas Bay and huddle beside a window of one of the seafront cafés, drinking coffee and watching the world go by. Severine ran upstairs and mentioned it to Raven, in case she wanted to go with them, but Raven declared she was staying put and pulled her duvet over her head to emphasise the point.

'Love you,' Severine said, kissing Raven through the duvet.

'Love you back,' came the reply.

Anxious that Raven may have seen or heard something at the party, Severine stayed a while longer.

'Did you have a good time last night?'

Raven threw back the cover. 'Brilliant! I can't believe how many people were there.' She propped herself up with her elbows. 'Robin Merry came. Did you see him? He was with his parents.'

Severine smiled and shook her head. 'Briefly, I think. But as you say, there were so many people, it was difficult to say hello to everyone. Did ... did your father have fun?'

Raven nodded. 'I think so. He said he did. He looked a bit fed up when we came home. He asked where you were when I went into the kitchen to have my hot chocolate, but I told him you were tired and had gone straight up to bed. Granny M and everyone asked about you, actually. I think they wanted to have a chat.'

'I expect they did. I'll catch up with them later. Are you sure you don't want to come out with Evie and me?'

Raven smiled and flopped back on her pillow, pulling the duvet back over her head. 'I'm sure,' she said. 'Have fun.'

Fun was the last thing Severine was expecting to have.

She crept back downstairs as quickly and as quietly as she could, using the other staircase to avoid being seen by anyone in the kitchen. Then she ran into reception where Evie was patiently waiting.

She and Evie, dressed appropriately for the weather, umbrellas in hand, made their way across the wooden bridge to the mainland of Snowflake Cove. They hurried past the row of cottages, in case anyone came out to chat about last night. Severine couldn't help but cast a quick glance at Jane's cottage, wondering if Logan sat inside, as confused and surprised by the turn of events at the party as she herself was.

'Don't even think about it,' Evie said, obviously reading Severine's mind.

'I'm trying not to.'

By the time the bus to Michaelmas Bay arrived, their hair was sodden, even beneath the shelter of their umbrellas, and they exchanged glances, both wondering whether this had been such a good idea, after all.

Thankfully, the bus was empty and it trundled up the hill from the village, passing through the winding lanes at the edge of Michaelmas Great Wood and the few houses scattered here and there, down the other side and into Michaelmas Bay without another single soul boarding.

'My treat,' Evie said, as they entered Beans and Leaves, one of Michaelmas Bay's best cafés – even if it did have a rather idiotic name.

'I'll get it,' Severine offered. 'I was the one who dragged you out for coffee.'

Evie threw her a look. 'Are we going to have an argument about this now? I'll get this. You get the next one. Go and grab a table by the window before it gets too crowded in here.'

Severine laughed. 'I don't think anyone else is stupid enough to come out in this weather.' But she headed to the table with the best view of the promenade and the marina beyond.

She and Evie were the only people there, and they had seen just one other person walking along the road, and that was probably because the dog that person was accompanying, needed a pee.

'I treated us to chocolate fudge cake, too.' Evie placed two plates, each one with a large slice of cake on it, on the table. 'It's an unwritten rule that rainy days require chocolate fudge cake to be eaten.'

'That's one rule I would never break.'

Evie smiled. 'You've broken all the others.'

The waitress brought the coffee over a mere matter of seconds later.

Severine rested her elbows on the table, her fork liberally piercing the chocolate cake topping.

'Did you understand any of what Gran said this morning?'

Evie sipped her coffee and shook her head. 'Not really. But I think the gist of it was that she doesn't believe you're deeply in love with Harvey. I wasn't sure if she was saying she thinks you're still in love with Roggero, or that you've fallen for Logan. Which I have to say, Severine, if you have, is a little bit weird. We've known him all our lives. If you've waited until you're engaged and pregnant by someone else to decide Logan is the man for you, your timing sucks.'

'That's the story of my life. Bad timing.'

'Or bad choices.'

Severine met her sister's look. 'Or both. Sprinkled with a bit of bad luck just to be sure.'

Evie laughed. 'I know it isn't funny, and I can't imagine what you're going through, but your love life does seem to be a bit of a disaster area. I hope mine doesn't turn out like that.'

'You've got Zachary. Your love life is going to be perfect.'

Evie beamed at her. 'You only met him yesterday. How can you be so sure?'

'Because I saw the way he looked at you. I hope you're going to ask me to be a bridesmaid.'

'We only started dating at Christmas. It's a bit premature to be thinking about bridesmaids.' She grinned. 'But now that you mention it, yes, and Raven and Juniper. So don't break Roggero's heart, or anything else of his, at least for the next year or two. I'd like all my bridesmaids to be on friendly terms.'

'The only one at risk of heartbreak is me. I can assure you of that.'

'Can you?' Evie took a bite of cake and quickly swallowed it. 'I saw Roggero looking at you more than once or twice last night.'

'He was probably wondering why he ever got involved with me.'

Evie shook her head in an exceptionally dramatic fashion. 'Nah uh. If anything, I would say that Roggero Tazzeone was wondering whether there was any possibility of getting involved with you again. Honestly. You should've seen the expression on his face when the Mayor put his arm around your waist. It was almost the same as the expression on the face of the Mayor's wife.' She grinned, showing her teeth, which were covered in chocolate.

'Stop messing around. He wasn't in the least bit bothered.'

Evie nodded. 'I think he was. Would you be interested?'

'Oh hell, I don't know. Everything was so clear before I came here. I was marrying Harvey. We were moving to New York. How can so much change in just one night? How can I have so many doubts? When I saw Roggero again after all these years, it was as if he had only walked away the day before. My heart nearly leapt out of my chest. Honestly. That's how I felt. Suddenly, I wanted to make him jealous. Why? For heaven's sake. So I kissed Logan. And then all I could think about was him. After just a couple of kisses in the moonlight.

Crazy, huh?' She shook her head. 'Why don't I know what I want?'

Evie shrugged. 'Search me. I suppose you could always put it down to your hormones. Or for want of anything better, you could … Blame it on the moonlight.'

'Oh very funny.'

Evie grinned. 'I'm serious, even though I may not look it. People do crazy things when the moon is reaching its full phase. Especially a moon like the one last night. So you'd better take care, because it reaches its peak in a couple of nights' time.'

'Great. I wonder what crazy thing I'll do next.'

'I don't know. But if I did, believe me, I'd start selling tickets.'

'Thanks for the support.'

'You're very welcome. Now eat your cake and then make up your mind whether it's Harvey, Logan, or Roggero who you want to grow old and wrinkled with.'

'If only it were that simple. We're chatting about this as if I'm choosing a pair of shoes or something equally as trivial.'

'I never thought I'd hear you say shoes were trivial.'

Severine smirked. 'You know what I mean. These are people. Men, made of flesh and blood. With feelings, hopes and dreams. I can't simply pick one and then toss him aside when I think I may prefer someone else.'

'And yet, that's exactly what you may need to do. If you want to be happy, that is.'

'Is it really that easy?'

'I didn't say it's going to be easy. And nor did Gran. But you can't go through life being miserable. You can't spend it with a man you only think you love, knowing that there's a man living his life without you. A man you really, truly love. A man you may have a chance to be with. Sometimes we have to take a risk. And sometimes we have to hurt someone to find our own happiness. And to help them find happiness of their own. Imagine how Harvey would feel if he discovered you'd rather be with someone else. That you were only marrying him because you thought you had gone too far down the track to halt the train you're on. He'd be as miserable as you would. I don't know what the answer is. I'm not sure I can be much help. But you need to give this thing some serious thought. And as much as you may not want to, I think you should discuss this with Mum and Dad, and also, let Raven know you're having doubts. Don't let her be the last to know what's going on. She may only be fifteen, but she notices more than she lets on.'

Severine took a mouthful of the delicious, gooey chocolate and closed her eyes whilst she savoured it. When she opened them again she said, 'Perhaps I'd be better off on my own, even though that thought terrifies me.'

'You'll never be on your own, Severine. You'll have Raven. And us. We may not always see eye to eye, and we may not agree with some of your choices, but the entire family loves you. Even Gran.'

'Oh well, if Gran loves me, life can't possibly be as bad as it seems.' Severine pulled a face. 'But you're right. And perhaps it is just my hormones.'

Evie shrugged. 'Perhaps. But personally, my money's on the moonlight.'

Chapter Twenty-Two

For the life of him, Roggero simply could not understand what was happening. He had not returned to Snowflake Cove for Severine. He had returned for Raven and her siblings. Other than a longing to know that Severine was safe and well and a sudden and uncomfortable feeling that life had moved on without him, he was sure his feelings for Severine were buried long ago. He had returned to find forgiveness for the huge mistakes of his past. And he had done that, to all intents and purposes. Sylvie still harboured some resentment, but that was to be expected. His children had exceeded all his hopes and dreams. They had forgiven him, if not entirely, then as near as was humanly possible. And for that alone he was truly thankful.

So why was he feeling like this? Why did he feel as if he might be about to lose everything?

He had found out at Christmas, when he'd returned to meet Raven and make amends, that Severine was engaged and about to be married. And not only that, he knew that she was expecting her fiancé's child. The news had hit him harder than he had expected, but he was glad that she was happy. Pleased that she had found love again.

He had known that Severine was coming home. He had known he would have to face her. He had never expected her to understand. Never thought for one moment that she would forgive him for what he had done. But he had also never thought that he would feel the way he did.

The moment he saw her, standing in the doorway of Snowflake Inn, he had felt it. Felt like a pilgrim must, when travelling for miles to view some holy relic, and finally being able to glimpse that revered object. All his life he had been searching for something, for someone, and yet when he had the chance for happiness – true happiness – he had not taken it. He had run away like a frightened, church mouse. To this day he had no idea why he had done that. No idea why he had stayed away.

He was convinced that it was in the past. That he no longer harboured strong feelings for Severine. But when he saw her standing there last night, it was as if the universe was giving him a second chance.

And if it was, he would take it.

It would not be easy, he knew that. There would be many problems to overcome. None of it made sense to him – and yet it felt so right.

Until he had seen Severine outside the restaurant with Logan.

Why had she kissed Logan?

Why had she done that?

Why had she rushed to her bedroom last night?

Was she avoiding him?

He was sure that there had been something in her eyes when she had looked at him before the party, standing by the door, anger flashing, mixed with a look he had seen so many times before, so long ago.

Was he mistaken?

Had it been no more than wishful thinking on his part?

He simply did not understand.

Was this merely his heart hankering for someone it knew it could not have?

Was that it?

Was this jealously?

Was this love?

After all these years and all the women he had known, was it even possible?

Did he still love Severine?

Could that be so? Could that happen?

And if he did, what of it?

She was engaged to another man. She was carrying another man's child.

Roggero did not understand what was happening. But he did understand one thing. He had to find out how he truly felt about Severine and if she felt anything for him.

Her fiancé was in New York.

She had come to Snowflake Cove and outside a restaurant in Michaelmas Bay, she had kissed Logan Dorset.

That must mean her feelings for her fiancé were not as strong and true as they should be. Perhaps she was not in love with her fiancé, after all.

But was she in love with Logan?

Or could she ever be in love again with him? Roggero Tazzeone, the man who had broken her heart so many years before.

Chapter Twenty-Three

Logan felt as if he were dancing on air. He could dance in the rain, like Gene Kelly had done in his gran's favourite film. But that would make him look stupid. What would people think if he danced with an umbrella, around a lamppost, and in rain-filled gutters?

Did he care?

He had kissed Severine. He had told her how he felt, after all these years.

And Severine had kissed him back.

All his dreams had come true in one glorious day. One glorious, moon-filled night. He did remember that. He did remember the moon. A huge, silver-white celestial ball throwing moonbeams and magic on to Michaelmas Bay and his restaurant.

Shit. He must be more hungover than he realised. He was getting all poetic and flowery. He grinned as he walked towards the car park. The grin turned to a smile as he glanced across at Snowflake Inn.

Should he go and say good morning to Severine? He should have asked for her mobile number. What an idiot he was not to have done that. What an idiot he was to have got so drunk last night. On his opening night, too. Did he do anything else embarrassing? Anything he shouldn't? Other than kiss the woman of his dreams, the woman who was another man's fiancée?

He cringed at the thought. Not the thought of kissing Severine. The thought of behaving like a shit. He believed he was a man with morals. Apparently, he was wrong. Last night he had behaved completely out of character. He didn't usually get drunk either. But he probably wouldn't have had the balls to kiss Severine if he had been sober. How had the kiss happened?

The last thing he could remember was looking at the moon after Zachary and his crew finished filming everyone standing outside the restaurant, for one of the segments for his show, 'Thorn On Your Side'.

Looking at the moon with Severine. And she had said something wonderful about the moon and his dad and the restaurant. What was that? What had she said?

No, wait. He hadn't been with Severine. It wasn't Severine who said those words. He was looking at the moon with someone else.

He was looking at the moon with Luna Blake.

'Logan!'

It was as if someone had thrown a bucket of iced water over him even though he was already half-soaked by the rain.

He looked across to the bridge and saw his mum closing in on him, calling his name as if she was about to read the Riot Act to him, which undoubtedly, she was. But it was more than that. He may not remember very much at all about last night but he did remember staring into Luna's eyes and feeling something he was sure he had never felt before. He remembered wanting to kiss her. A woman he'd met just a few hours earlier. He definitely remembered that.

So why had he kissed Severine?

And where was Luna when he had?

'Logan. You and I need to talk.'

'Hi, Mum. Yes, I'm sure we do, but can it wait? I'm having trouble remembering what happened last night and I need to clear my head. I need to think it through.'

'Well, I can fill in some of the details, if you like.' From her tone, she wasn't pleased.

'I'm not sure that would help.'

'I'm not offering to help. I would rather like an explanation. But I'm not having this discussion in the rain. We're going back to Jane's.'

'I need to get to the restaurant.'

'Fine. Then we'll have this conversation there.' She glared at him. 'You weren't thinking of driving, were you? After the amount of alcohol you had last night, I hardly think that's wise. We'll take my car. Unlike you, I only had one drink.'

'Great. Thanks.'

Logan no longer felt like dancing in the rain. And he had an uneasy feeling that this was going to be a very long, and rather unpleasant day.

Chapter Twenty-Four

Severine was not particularly looking forward to lunch. All her family would be there, and no doubt Roggero, too. She and Evie had spent a lovely morning in Michaelmas Bay, all things considered and when they returned, they had both headed back to their room, where Raven had joined them. They played a game of Monopoly, whilst the rain lashed against the windows and the DJ on Michaelmas Music FM played every song with rain connotations. Severine was enjoying herself, until *New York Raining* by Charles Hamilton drifted into the room. It was one of Harvey's favourites and without a moment's warning, Severine burst into tears.

'Mum! What's wrong?' Raven wrapped an arm around Severine's shoulders.

Severine shook her head and wept on to Raven's hand-knitted jumper that had been one of Raven's Christmas presents from Jessie.

'I think it's the song,' Evie said.

Raven listened to the words for a second or two and nodded.

'Oh, I get it. You're missing Harvey.'

Severine choked on a sob and Evie slapped her on the back.

'Thanks,' Severine said through her tears.

'You're welcome,' Evie replied.

Severine wiped her eyes with the sleeve of her cardigan and smiled at Raven.

'I'm sorry darling. I don't know why that hit me so hard. My emotions are all over the place. I'm fine now though.'

'You're pregnant, Mum. That happens, doesn't it?' She looked across at Evie.

Evie shrugged. 'Don't ask me.' She grinned at Raven. 'I still think it's got something to do with the moon.'

'Huh?' Raven looked out of the window. 'It's daylight. OK, it's as black as a crow's armpit out there, but there isn't any sign of the moon.'

Evie threw the dice. 'Just because you can't see it, doesn't mean it's not there. I watched a documentary about the moon, once. You'd be amazed by the power it has on us.' She moved her cat piece eight spaces and picked up a Chance card. 'Rats. I've got to go straight to jail. Do not pass Go. Do not collect £200.' She placed the card on the bottom of the pile. 'Do crows have armpits? Wouldn't they be wingpits?'

Severine laughed. 'You're a wingpit.'

'I'm hungry,' Raven said. 'Perhaps that's what's wrong, Mum. Perhaps you're hungry. I'm gonna see if lunch is ready.'

She jumped to her feet but instead of running downstairs as Severine expected, Raven grabbed her phone off the bed where she'd tossed it, and texted someone. A second later, her phone pinged a reply.

'Lunch will be on the table in less than five minutes.'

Severine grinned. 'Have we run out of plates?' She laughed at her own joke.

Evie grinned and pulled a face. 'And the old Severine is back. Finally.'

'Huh?' Raven said. 'Oh. I get it. You should be on the stage, Mum.'

The three of them headed down to the kitchen where Jessie and John were already seated at the table. Jessie had insisted on using some of her new wealth to bolster the number of employees and Molly was checking with one of the new staff members that all the guests had finished their lunches and the plates had been cleared away.

'That's good. Do you want to join us for lunch?' Molly asked Jeanette.

Jeanette smiled. 'No ta. I'm meeting me mam in Michaelmas Bay. It's my afternoon off.'

'Of course it is.' Molly smiled and patted Jeanette's arm. 'Have fun. See you tomorrow.'

'See ya.' Jeanette waved at everyone and winked at Raven as she walked out.

'There you are, Severine,' Jessie said. 'I believe your mother wants a word.'

Molly tutted at Jessie. 'Now is hardly the time, is it?'

Raven pulled out a chair. 'Mum's feeling a bit emotional.'

Jessie raised her brows. 'I expect she is.'

John glared at Jessie. 'Not in front of Raven, Mum.'

'What?' Raven asked, looking from her grandad to Jessie and then Severine. 'Have I missed something? What's going on?'

'Nothing, darling,' Molly said, sending a warning look to Jessie. 'Your mum and I just need to have a little chat about a few things, that's all. We'll do that after lunch. Won't we, Severine?'

Severine nodded grudgingly at Molly. 'Yes, Mum.'

'Good,' Jessie said. 'Let's tuck in. There's nothing quite like steak and mushroom pie, mashed potato and baked beans on a rainy day like today.'

John looked at Jessie and grinned. 'Don't eat too many baked beans, Mum, or it'll be a windy and rainy day.'

'You're not too old for me to give you a clip around the ear, my lad.'

Severine smiled. Lunch wasn't going to be too bad, after all. But this afternoon may be a different matter.

Chapter Twenty-Five

Luna wasted most of the morning, giving herself lectures on the stupidity of falling for a handsome face. Had she learnt nothing from her experience with Mateus?

Apparently not. Which was a great pity because she had paid a very high price for that particular lesson in love. Not just in financial terms. The man had also broken her heart. But perhaps that hadn't taken much. Her heart hadn't had time to mend from her dad's death, and it hadn't even begun to heal from her mum's when Mateus wheedled his way into it.

He told her he loved her.

He lied. He cheated on her behind her back, and finally left one night whilst she slept. He had done what her dad would have called, a *moonlight flit*. Rather ironic, given Luna's love of all things associated with moonlight. He had taken the money she kept in the house. Taken all the money they had saved in the joint account that he had suggested they open. An account that only she had added to, it seemed. Luckily, the house was in her sole name, having been left to her by her parents. And he hadn't touched their artwork, or any of hers. He'd also left the jewellery and other items of value. Mateus only wanted cash – and he'd taken plenty of it. Several thousand pounds.

The police were called, but there was little they could do. It was a joint account, and she had no proof that there was cash in the house. No point in claiming on the insurance either. She continued working as a waitress in the local, English-owned, Tapas Bar and wondered about her future. It had been looking pretty bleak until Mason asked if she wished to remain in Spain.

'I have a spare room,' he said, during one of their phone conversations. 'Why don't you come and stay for a while? Or better still, if you're considering leaving Spain, why not return to England and come and live with me? You can stay forever. Or just until you find your feet. I'll be happy either way.'

She thought it was merely something he felt he should say, but each time they spoke after that, he reminded her of the offer. She put the house on the market, to test the waters, and got an immediate offer. She had used what little money she had saved since Mateus had left, and gone to Norway for Christmas to visit a friend and to fulfil a lifelong dream to photograph the Northern Lights.

On her return, she had packed her parents' artwork, organised international shippers to collect the crates and the few items of furniture with sentimental value, and sent them on their way. The day the house sale completed, she packed her case, boarded the plane to Gatwick and told herself that this was the beginning of a new adventure.

Some adventure. She'd only been here one day, and already she had made a dumb mistake. She'd fallen for another handsome face.

So what? There was no real harm done, was there? She would erase all thoughts of Logan Dorset from her mind. She would concentrate on her career. This was a fresh start and she would make this work. She would spend her days painting and her nights taking photos of the moon. She would get to know people and make some friends. She would wander the narrow streets of Michaelmas Bay and search all the nooks and crannies. She would take long walks in Michaelmas Great Wood, or along the beaches of the Bay. But maybe not today.

She peered out the window at the torrential rain. Today was not a day for walking. Today was the sort of day to curl up in front of the fire with a good book and a hot drink.

A hot man would be better.

Stop it. Stop. It!

Anyone would think she was man mad. It must be a combination of the effects of too much alcohol last night and the never-ending rain today.

Despite the weather, what she needed was some exercise.

Mason was snoring softly in his chair beside the fire, his book dangling like a heavy leaf from his branch-like arm. He looked so peaceful that she didn't want to wake him.

She wrote him a note and took the book from his hand, placing the note and his glasses on the small, circular table next to his chair. She grabbed her large tote bag, slipped her camera inside, threw on her coat and gently closed the front door of Bell Cottage behind her.

Juniper, the neighbour whom she'd met last night, waved at her from her doorway. Juniper and her partner, Darren were friends of Evie Starr, whom she'd also met at the party, along with Evie's famous boyfriend, the TV star and ex-SAS officer, Zachary Thorn. Now there was a man to get a girl's heart racing. Not that he was really Luna's type. Nice to look at though.

'How are you today?' Juniper yelled. 'Darren's still in bed with a sore head and I've only been up for about twenty minutes. Where are you off to in this grim weather?' She bent down to pick up two bottles of milk from the doorstep.

Did people still have milk delivered? Clearly they did.

She smiled at Juniper. 'I'm fine, thanks. Sorry about Darren. I don't suppose he's the only one. I'm going to get the bus into town, I think. I need some fresh air.'

'Rather you than me. It's really tipping it down. D'you fancy a coffee. I've got the kettle on.' She waggled the milk bottles in her hand.

Luna hesitated for a split second. Didn't she decide just now that she needed to make some friends?

'I'd love a coffee, if you're sure it's not too much trouble.'

Juniper laughed. 'Why would it be that? I wouldn't have offered if it was. Oh. It's instant. Is that OK? I hope you weren't expecting some of that freshly ground coffee bean stuff.'

Luna laughed too. 'Nope. Instant is great. Thanks.'

She followed Juniper inside. The cottage was similar in size to Mason's, or so she thought, until the hall led into a massive kitchen extension at the back. Everything was sleek and glossy white, lit by large chrome lamps hanging from a white oak beam. What little daylight there was flooded in via bi-fold glass doors and a large, glass roof. As an artist, Luna adored this space, especially as it faced north. It was pretty spectacular as a kitchen.

'Gosh! What a fantastic room.'

Juniper beamed. 'Darren gave it to me for Christmas. Not the room, the kitchen. Although he did give me the room too, because he had this extension built and the glass windows and doors put in. We didn't think it would be finished so soon, what with all the bad weather we've had. In fact we were astonished when they started, but the builders enclosed the site with special sheeting and we had heaters on full-time. The new walls are solid wood. American white oak, and they were built off-site and fitted together. It's amazing what they can do these days. You should've seen it before. It was as dark as a cave, and just as damp as one when we were cooking in here. This is my dream kitchen.'

'I can see why. It would be my dream kitchen too.'

'It's actually got one of those fancy, built-in hot taps, but I still can't get used to using it. I automatically boil the kettle. I'm such an idiot at times.'

'I'm hopeless with any modern equipment. It took me ages to figure out how to use all the knobs and buttons on the coffee machine in the local Tapas Bar where I worked as a waitress. And that wasn't modern by these standards.' She scanned the sleek line of cupboards and spotted the polished steel of the massive cooker. 'That looks like something from another galaxy.'

'Tell me about it.' Juniper pulled a face as she made coffee. 'It looked fab in the magazine – and it still does – but I think you need a degree in engineering or rocket science or something to work the thing. Don't tell Darren I said that. I had to Google it to find out how to turn the oven on.' She handed Luna a mug and nodded towards the white granite table and the white and chrome chairs. 'Take a seat. So what did you think of Logan and his restaurant? Fab, huh?'

Luna almost spilt her coffee. That would've been a great start to this new friendship. Coffee stains on a white, padded velvet seat would not have gone down well.

'Yes. Fab.'

Juniper sipped her coffee and observed Luna over the rim. She laughed.

'That's it? Either you're a woman of few words, or you didn't have as much fun as Darren and I did last night. Didn't you enjoy it?'

Luna nodded. 'Very much. I think the restaurant is something really special and I'm sure it'll be a great success. But there were so many people there and I definitely had too much to drink. On top of that, and the journey from Spain yesterday, I think I was a bit overwhelmed to really take much in.'

'Someone told me those were your photos and paintings on the walls. Is that true? Are you an artist?'

'Yes. My passion is the moon, so virtually all of my art involves the moon, or moonlight in some shape or form.'

'That's pretty handy considering the restaurant is called Moonlight. What an incredible coincidence?'

'And a fortunate one for me. I want to see if I can earn a living from my art. Having my pictures on display in Log … in the restaurant is a dream opportunity.'

Juniper gave her a curious look. Had she noticed the way Luna had avoided saying that man's name?

'This is the perfect place to sell artwork,' Juniper said. 'Not so much at this time of year but from Easter onwards, Snowflake Cove and Michaelmas Bay are packed to the gills with tourists. You could sell your pictures from Mason's front door.'

Luna laughed. 'That sounds like heaven. I could sit outside, like the women in our village did, and have my pictures lined up against the wall.'

Juniper laughed too. 'You could sit outside for possibly three days during the summer. The rest of the time you'll be shivering if you do. You'll soon be wishing you were back in Spain. Oh, sorry. That wasn't very tactful, was it? Jane told us your parents have both passed away and that you've recently split from your boyfriend. She said you were coming here to make a fresh start.'

'Jane told you?'

Juniper grinned. 'Yeah. You'd better get used to that. Jane Dorset – and Jessie Starr – know every single thing that goes on in this village, and if they don't, then it's probably not worth knowing. You must've met Jessie last night. She was probably saying something scathing to someone. She's one of those people who says

163

exactly what she wants. Deep down, she's lovely though. She's my best friend, Evie's gran. I know you met Evie and Zach last night.'

'Yes. And I met Evie's sister Severine on the train from Gatwick yesterday. Although I didn't realise who she was until my uncle told me.'

Juniper sipped her coffee and raised her brows before she spoke again.

'Ah yes. The lovely Severine. No drama would be complete without Severine. She's a bit of a … how can I say this politely?' She shrugged. 'I can't. Severine is a bit of a cow and I can say that from first-hand experience.'

'Really?'

Juniper nodded. 'Oh yes. She had an affair with my dad. He was also there last night. The tall, dark, handsome Italian-looking guy. He's only been back since Christmas. Severine got herself pregnant and Dad did a runner rather than face the consequences, and my mum. We hadn't heard a word from him for years. But listen to me going on. You'll think I'm a lunatic.'

'No, I won't.'

'Jane will probably tell you all about it anyway, if she hasn't already. Or maybe Mason has. But he's not as much of a gossip, is he? Not like Jane. You know he's got a bit of a thing for Jane, don't you? Of course you do. He's your uncle. Anyway. All I'll say about Severine is watch out. She can be nice, but she's much better at being a bitch. I pity the man she's got her claws into now. *Harvey*.

God. I sound like a bitch myself. Would you like a biscuit? I'm sure I've got some somewhere.'

'No thanks. I'm fine. Um. How long has Severine been with Harvey?'

'Not long. I think they were going out for a few months before she discovered she was pregnant. They got pretty serious, very fast. She'd gone to New York for the holidays to meet his folks. She called from Las Vegas to say they were getting married, which went down with the Starrs like a boat with a hole in its bottom, let me say. Especially with Raven. She's Severine's daughter – and my half-sister. The stunning girl with long black hair. She was wearing a pink dress at the party.'

Luna nodded. 'I remember her. She is stunning. You're very alike.'

Juniper grinned. 'We're not, but thanks for the compliment. I take after Mum. My brother Roly takes after Dad. What was I saying? Oh yeah. Severine. They postponed the wedding and Severine was supposed to come home for New Year, but she didn't. We were beginning to wonder if we'd ever see her again to be honest. But she wouldn't leave Raven. Even though Severine's a cow, she does love Raven, in her own, selfish, self-absorbed way. I think you can tell, I don't like Severine very much. My friend Evie is the complete opposite. She would do anything for anyone. And she would never steal someone else's husband, partner or boyfriend. Severine would

165

steal all three, and still have time to find someone new. More coffee?'

'Yes please.' Without hesitation Luna asked: 'Does anyone around here like Severine? Other than her family, of course.'

Juniper refilled their mugs and resumed her seat. 'I don't think so. Oh wait. Evie said something to me at Christmas. I think it was about Logan. Yes. Yes it was. But she said that Severine used to have a crush on Logan, I think. She didn't say what Logan thought of Severine. From memory, he seemed to avoid her when we were kids. Logan's only just come back here too. It's funny really. Everyone seems to be coming back after years away. Ooh! If you're on the look out for a new man, you might consider Logan. He's hot – and he cooks. That's a pretty good start.'

This time Luna did spill her coffee, but luckily, it was only on the table. Juniper wiped it up in a flash.

'Sorry, Juniper. My mug slipped in my fingers.'

'Not a problem.' She winked at Luna. 'Thinking about hot men like Logan can do that to a girl.'

'I wasn't …' Luna's voice trailed off.

What was the point in lying? She'd thought about little else except Logan Dorset since she spotted him at the station. It was time she set her mind on something else. Or if absolutely necessary, *someone* else. Logan Dorset couldn't be the only single man around here, could he? Perhaps a fling with no strings attached was what she needed. She was definitely missing sex. Mateus may have been a liar and a cheat, but where sex was concerned, the man knew what he was doing. Not quite a gift from the gods, perhaps, but he would certainly be able to keep a woman happy on a wet and cloudy day like this.

Chapter Twenty-Six

Severine's chat with her mum had not been nearly as bad as she had expected. In fact, it had all gone rather well. The only fly in the ointment had been the fact that Jessie had insisted on being there too. Not that Jessie said a great deal – and that was a miracle in itself – other than to agree with virtually every statement or piece of advice that Molly uttered. And that was probably because Molly said much the same as Jessie had done earlier.

'All we want is for you to be happy,' Molly said, reaching out across the kitchen table and taking Severine's hand in hers. 'Jessie told your father and me about your earlier conversation, and John and I agree. Whatever you want to do, we'll support you one hundred per cent. But the thing is, darling, you don't seem exactly sure what that is. You obviously need time to think about it, and that's fine with us. What we don't want is for you to rush into something and then have regrets. Why don't you speak to Harvey and tell him that you plan to stay here for a while?'

'How long is a while?'

'That's entirely up to you. Weeks. Months. Years.'

'Years? Our baby is due in the summer. I think I need to make a decision long before that, don't you?'

Molly shook her head. 'Not if you're still unsure. And you are unsure, aren't you, darling?'

Severine nodded. 'I wasn't until yesterday. I thought I knew exactly what I wanted. Who I wanted. Now …' She shrugged and shook her head.

'Love is very strange sometimes. We think we know what our heart wants and then suddenly it shows us it wants something else entirely. Something we had never even thought of until our heart jumps up and down and does a little dance and yells, 'Him. I want him!' That's when we know. Our heart is often right. But not always. Sometimes our heart gets it wrong.'

'So how do I decide? How do I know? I love Harvey. I'm sure I do. And yet …'

'Don't over think it, darling. That's my advice. Just take each day as it comes and one day you'll know. Believe me. You will.'

Jessie smiled. 'Listen to your mother, Severine. And listen to me. You're a Starr. And a Starr's heart has never led them wrong. We've all had handsome men thrown in our path but we've always picked the best. Maybe not in looks. Perhaps not in wealth. But always the best for us.'

'I haven't done too well so far, have I? Don't answer that. Tell me instead, what handsome men have been in your life then? Was Joshua Thorn one of them? I haven't heard the full story about him yet. Are you going to tell me?'

Jessie looked her in the eye. 'I suppose it's only fair.' She shifted in her chair. 'Put the kettle on again Molly, there's a dear. You've heard the story anyway.'

Molly smiled. 'I'll make us all some more tea.'

'Come on then, Gran. Spill the beans.'

Jessie gazed into the distance as if her life was playing out before her like a film.

'Joshua and your grandfather were friends since birth. Joshua's family lived nearby in those days. I was fifteen when I came here and I fell in love with William Starr the minute I saw him. He was cleaning mud from a horse's hoof and looked up as I approached. Then, as now, they used a horse and cart to cross the bridge to this inn. I knew in that second that he was the person I was going to marry. He told me later that he had felt exactly the same about me. I didn't meet Joshua until a few weeks later and William and I were courting by then. You might find this hard to believe, looking at me now, but I was a pretty little thing. Joshua Thorn liked pretty things.' She tutted. 'He still does. But anyway. He wanted me the moment he saw me.'

'So Joshua fell in love with you at first sight too?'

'Did I say love? It wasn't love. Although he says it was. I said he wanted me. And even in those days, Joshua Thorn expected to get what he wanted. The man wouldn't take no for an answer. Oh, he didn't force himself on me or anything so disgusting, but he wouldn't leave me alone. Every time I turned around, the man was there. Buying me presents, whispering things in my ear, trying to undermine William in my affections. I told him that nothing would ever entice me to choose him over William. That there was nothing he could do or say to make me change my mind.'

'Did Grandad know what his so-called friend was up to?'

Jessie shook her head. 'No. William loved Joshua Thorn like a brother. It never occurred to him for one minute that Joshua might try to steal his girl. And as angry as Joshua made me, I couldn't tell William his best friend was betraying him behind his back.'

'So what happened? Why did Joshua owe you money? Why did he give you that massive IOU at Christmas?'

'I'll tell you, if you'll stop interrupting.'

Severine grinned and both she and Jessie sipped the tea Molly had poured for them.

'William and Joshua had started a business together. William seemed to be the one who did all the work. Joshua was the one who had got them the finances they needed. Even then, Joshua had a magic touch with money, whereas William seemed to have a pocket with a hole in as far as money was concerned. It was only sensible to let Joshua handle that side of things, or so we thought. They started the business shortly after the war. William's family owned this place and William and Joshua began buying small hotels and inns and turning them into the sort of establishments that would appeal to the middle classes. People didn't go abroad in those days and they didn't have six weeks holiday a year.'

'I don't get six weeks holiday now. And Mum certainly doesn't. Sorry. I didn't mean to interrupt.'

Jessie smiled. 'I'll cut it short. Joshua said they should set their sights higher. This was a time when stately homes were going for a song. They were being pulled down, or sold off. No one wanted the burden of them. Joshua told us he was ploughing every penny back into the business, paying himself and us just enough to live on. What he didn't tell us was that what he needed to live on was far greater than our requirements. He bought himself a house in London, unbeknown to us. And later, properties abroad. None of which appeared on the books. I don't know how he did it. I'm not sure that I care. But he cheated William and me out of a fortune.'

'So how did you find out?'

'We didn't. Not until much later, by which time William and Joshua had parted company. Joshua had persuaded William into some bad investments and money became tight for us. Joshua's finances appeared to be healthy and William asked him for a loan. Joshua refused. Instead he offered to buy William out of the business. He gave us a valuation and William trusted him. Joshua said – and he still maintains this – that in the market at the time it was a fair price. But he didn't include any of the properties he had bought with his own substantially higher salary. As I said, William was not the best with money. We soon found ourselves with just this inn. But even so, we were happy. We saw less and less of Joshua. Until one day he turned up at this door and told me that he could take me away from this. He told me just how rich he was. And that's when I knew he had cheated us, but of course I couldn't prove it and William would not believe me.'

'Do you think he planned it? Planned to make Grandad poor in the hope that you would leave him?'

'Yes. That's precisely what I thought. I hated Joshua then. He tells me now that there was no plan. That he just hoped. I'm not sure I'm convinced. And he definitely cheated us. Why else would he give me all this money now?'

'It was an IOU, wasn't it? So he knew he owed you money. He's admitted it.'

'He says it's out of guilt for paying himself much more than he paid William for all those years. But he says that William knew. Perhaps he did. I'll never know now. But I took the money and I'm glad of it.'

Molly smiled. 'And so are we. Without it we wouldn't be here now. Things were very grim financially for us. Like it or not, Joshua Thorn was an answer to our prayers.'

'Were things really that bad?' Severine had no idea.

Jessie nodded. 'John is not as bad with money as his father was, but yes, things were fairly grim. Or at the very least they were certainly not looking good.'

'Gosh. And what about Joshua? Have you seen him since Christmas?'

'Once or twice. He wants us to be friends. I'm considering it. Not because I like him, but because, somehow, I feel that is what William would have wanted. In spite of everything.'

Raven appeared in the kitchen doorway. 'What are you three chatting about?'

'Money,' said Severine.

'Friendship,' Molly said.

Jessie sighed. 'Love, Raven. We're talking about love.'

Chapter Twenty-Seven

Luna caught the bus into Michaelmas Bay almost an hour later than she had planned. Jane Dorset may be the village gossip, but Juniper Green came a very close second. Luna now knew something about everyone who lived in Snowflake Cove, and several of the residents of Michaelmas Bay. She made a mental note never to divulge any secrets to Juniper, unless they were secrets Luna wanted people to know.

Rain still pelted the village and, apart from Luna, there was only one other passenger on the bus. She didn't know where she was going but the High Street seemed as good a place as any to start, so that was the destination she had given to the driver when she boarded.

'This is the High Street, love,' he informed her several minutes later. 'Unless you want the end that comes out at the marina?'

'No,' she said, remembering that Logan's restaurant overlooked the marina. 'This end is fine.'

Stepping off the bus and opening her umbrella, she looked around her. There were clothes shops, gift shops, a couple of card shops, a bookshop and a small, department store. She could see a couple of cafés and a cocktail-cum-wine bar that looked rather inviting. But she had probably consumed enough alcohol last night to keep her going for a week. She wasn't looking for anything in particular, so she ambled down the street, window-shopping as she went. Hearing the footsteps of someone running behind her, she glanced over her shoulder to check she wasn't in the way, and careered into something solid, knocking her backwards.

'Shit. Sorry. Are you OK?' a man's voice asked, as a firm hand grabbed her arm to support her. 'I wasn't looking where I was going.'

Luna peered up at him from beneath her umbrella and let out a little gasp.

'Um. Neither was I. I heard someone behind me.'

No sooner had she said that than another man pounded by, throwing her a friendly smile, water dripping from his dark-blond hair.

'Him,' she said, pointing at the runner disappearing around the corner.

'Yes,' the first man said. 'That's Ian.'

'You know him?'

The man grinned. 'It's a small town.'

So the runner wasn't smiling at her, he was smiling at this man.

'Not as small as Snowflake Cove.'

His grin widened. 'Nowhere is as small as Snowflake Cove. I'm Chris. Hello.'

'Hello. I'm Luna. And that's a rather sweeping statement. How do you know that nowhere is as small?' She returned his grin.

'Luna? Doesn't that mean Moon? That's an unusual name. There's a restaurant around the corner called Moonlight.'

'Yes. I was at the opening party last night.'

'Were you? So was I. How did I miss seeing you? And to answer your question, I don't know if anywhere is smaller. But I can't imagine it, can you?'

'Were you really there last night?'

'Yes.' He tilted his head slightly and narrowed his eyes, but the mischievous grin remained. 'Were *you* really there?'

'I was.'

'Wait a minute. Are you Luna, as in Luna Blake?' He tutted. 'Of course you are. Why am I even asking? There couldn't be two Lunas in Michaelmas Bay. So you're an artist?'

'Yes. And you are…?'

'Impressed.'

'I meant, what do you do?'

He grinned. 'I do all sorts of things. But for my day job, I work in Michaelmas Bay

Books.' He pointed to the other side of the road and beyond.

'The bookshop?'

'Yes. The clue was in the name.'

'You should be a comedian.'

'Funny you should say that. That's what I moonlight as.'

'Oh ha ha.' Luna made a face with a silly smile.

He laughed. 'I'm serious. I work as a comedian one night a week. But I'm the first to admit, I'm not very good at it. Why are we standing in the rain?'

'Because it's raining.'

'Funny woman. What *I meant* was, if we're going to have a conversation why don't we have it over coffee?'

'Oh.'

'I can tell from your expression that's not a thrilling prospect.'

'No. I mean yes. I was just surprised.'

'So that's a yes?'

Luna nodded. Possibly a little too enthusiastically. 'Yes.'

'Great. I've been standing here for hours waiting for someone to come along so that I could bump into them and get them to buy me a coffee. As a struggling bookseller and a second-rate comedian, I can't afford to buy my own.'

'Oh. OK.'

He shook his head and laughed. 'That was a joke. Now you know what a crap comedian I am.' He took her by the hand. 'I'm buying. The café is this way.' He nodded his head in the direction of the marina.

'Oh.' Luna held back, surprised at the way he had taken her hand as if it were the most natural thing in the world to do. But she also hesitated because Logan Dorset's restaurant was in that direction and she had a vague recollection from last night, that to get to any of the cafés on the marina, they would have to pass Moonlight, Logan's restaurant. As foolish as it was, she didn't relish that prospect.

'Is something wrong? Have you changed your mind?'

'How do I know you're not a serial killer?'

He let go of her hand and crossed his heart. 'I swear I have never hurt a cornflake in my life.'

'That's a terrible joke.'

'I'm a terrible comedian. So, yes or no to coffee? I can give you my mum's phone number, if that might help. She'll tell you what a lovely young man I am. I always give her as my alibi.' He grinned again. 'Sorry. I'll stop now.'

'OK,' Luna said. 'But if you kill me, I'll never forgive you. Don't you have to work this afternoon?'

He shook his head. 'I own the bookshop and it just so happens this is my afternoon off.'

'That's handy.'

'Yes. I decided that about a minute ago.' He took her hand again. 'We're running. I don't want you to trip.'

'Why are we running?'

'I need the exercise.'

Luna laughed, and they ran towards the marina, jumping over puddles on the way, their two umbrellas bashing against one another like dodgem cars at a fair and sending little waterfalls of rain pouring to the ground.

Chapter Twenty-Eight

Logan sat at one of the tables in the two bow windows of Moonlight, supposedly planning menus for the week ahead, but in reality, staring out of the window at the rain and the boats bobbing on the choppy waters of Michaelmas Bay. His mum had given him an even sterner talking to than his gran had done, and he had gone from feeling elated to deflated rather quicker than he had hoped. He had never expected the feeling of euphoria he experienced on discovering that he had finally kissed Severine and told her how he felt, to last, but he thought it might at least survive the day. His mum, his gran and even, apparently, Molly Starr, all had other ideas. No one apart from him, it seemed, felt that there was any chance of a relationship working out between himself and Severine.

'It's not that I don't like Severine,' his mum had said. 'But your gran and I both agree that you simply aren't right for one another.'

'I'm a grown man, Mum. I think I should be allowed to decide who is or isn't right for me.'

'Of course. And you know that I would never usually interfere in your affairs. No pun intended. Perhaps I should say, your love life. But Severine is engaged and carrying another man's child. On top of that, she already has one child by someone else's husband.'

'Sylvie and Roggero were never married.'

'Don't nitpick, darling. You know what I mean. She had an affair with someone else's partner. She doesn't exactly have a good track record as far as relationships are concerned. I want you to be happy. Your gran wants you to be happy. Your father would want you to be happy. Rest his soul. What do you think he would be saying to you if he were sitting here instead of me?'

Logan had glared at his mum. 'That's a low blow, Mum. Bringing Dad into this. But you know what, I think Dad would simply say that if this was what I wanted, what I really wanted, then I should go for it. And I think he would wish me the best of luck. I've loved Severine all my life, Mum. Don't you get that? No one else has ever replaced her. I've never felt about any of the women I've dated, the way I feel about her. Don't you think I would rather be with someone less complicated, less … difficult, if I had a choice? But I don't. Yes, she has faults. Yes, she has history. But we all have faults. We all have some history. But can't you see, that in spite of that, I still love her. Surely that means something?'

'Are you really hoping for a future with her? Do you honestly believe there's a chance of that? Even Molly, her own mother, thinks that Severine made a mistake last night. That Severine will end up hurting you. None of us want that. And are you really prepared to be some sort of surrogate father to both Raven and this new baby? Don't you want children of your own? You've just started a new business, Logan. You could have a bright future ahead of you. Do you really want to mess it up over a woman? I can't bear the thought of her breaking your heart.'

Logan digested everything his mother had said. He took her hand and squeezed it.

'Firstly, Mum, I don't know if Severine and I have a future together. All I know is I love her and that I have to take this chance. Secondly, I don't care if Molly, or anyone else, thinks Severine made a mistake last night. I only care what Severine thinks. If she thinks it was a mistake then so be it.' He shrugged. 'Thirdly, Raven's a great kid. She has a father, and as Roggero is planning on sticking around, I don't think Raven needs me to be her dad. But if she does, that's fine. I'll be her dad or her friend. Whatever she needs. As for the new baby, yes, I'll happily be whatever Severine wants me to be. And as for wanting kids of my own, yes, of course I do. But that won't stop me from treating both Raven and the new baby as my own, either. Instead of fighting this, why can't everyone just leave me and Severine alone so that we can sort this out. I kissed her. I told her I loved her. Apparently. But we didn't set a date for our wedding, or anything. Don't you think that everyone might just be jumping the gun a little?'

She looked him in the eye and smiled, letting out a long, low sigh. 'I suppose you're right, darling. After all, it was just a couple of kisses in the moonlight. And you did have rather a lot to drink. I'm sure when you think things through, and get a chance to talk to Severine, it will all sort itself out. I really hope so, anyway. And you know I'm only saying all of this because I love you so much. You're a wonderful young man, Logan. Hard-working, loyal and honest. I know in my heart that somewhere out there, there's a young woman who is absolutely perfect for you and who will make you very happy. I also know in my heart, that woman is not Severine Starr. But I won't say anything else on the subject. Not today, anyway. Now I'd better let you get on. You've got a restaurant run.'

Since his mother had left, Logan had done nothing but think things through.

He loved Severine. He always had. From a very young age he had put her on a pedestal and worshipped her. Severine could do no wrong in his eyes. He knew all of her faults, and loved her more because of them. He had always imagined that he could be the man to change her from the often moody, often selfish, sometimes unpleasant and uncaring woman she was, into the loving, selfless, caring and delightful woman he knew she could be. The woman he was sure she wanted to be. All she needed was the right man to love her.

He sat at the table and peered out the window, watching the rain, and the boats bobbing in the marina as a couple ran in front of the restaurant, hand in hand, jumping puddles and laughing. He watched them run to one of the café's situated diagonally opposite his restaurant, and close their umbrellas in the doorway.

As the man turned, Logan saw it was Chris Lyons, the owner of Michaelmas Bay Books.

Since when had Chris had a girlfriend? He hadn't brought her to the party last night.

Chris stepped to one side and opened the café door. The woman went inside and a few seconds later, stood next to one of the tables in the window, glancing in the direction of Logan's restaurant.

Their eyes met through the rain and the two sets of glass, and the short distance between them.

It was Luna. The woman who had been holding hands and running in the rain, with Chris, was Luna.

Had they met last night? Had she gone inside, after standing with Logan in the moonlight and looking into each other's eyes? Had she gone inside and met Chris? Had she gone inside and arranged a date with another man?

What was he getting so upset about? Why did it bother him? He should be wishing her well. Wishing them both well.

After all, he had only met Luna himself, yesterday. Why did it matter that she had met someone else? He didn't have feelings for her.

He was in love with Severine. He'd been in love with Severine his entire life. And finally, he'd kissed her and told her how he felt. He'd wanted to do that for longer than he cared to remember.

He was definitely in love with Severine.

He absolutely was.

He was.

Wasn't he?

Chapter Twenty-Nine

Roggero spotted Severine the moment she walked into the bar, which was virtually empty save for one or two diehards who had battled through the rain in order to have a drink at their favourite inn. She obviously spotted him too, because she quickly turned and walked back out.

Putting his half-drunk pint of beer on the table in front of him, he got up and followed her.

She stopped at the lounge door, hesitated and walked away.

He followed her as she pushed open one door of the dining room and walked through to the other side, opening another door leading into the reception, where she turned, crossed her arms in front of her and waited for him to catch her up.

'Are you following me?' She scowled at him.

He glared at her. 'Yes. Are you avoiding me?'

'Yes. But you've been avoiding me all day.'

'I have not been avoiding you. I have been thinking.'

'Really? What do you want? A fanfare?' She clapped her hands. 'Yay! Roggero Tazzeone has been thinking.'

'And Severine Starr has been kissing men who are not her fiancé.' He clapped his hands too.

She glowered at him. 'One man! I only kissed one man.'

'But a man who is not your fiancé.'

'So what? What business is it of yours who I kiss? What right do you have to question what I do?'

'It is not my business. I have no right. I know this. And yet here I am.'

'And? What does that mean? "Here I am.". I can see you. I'm not blind.'

'I am not blind either. I can see you. I can see you are not happy. You should be happy, Severine. You deserve to be.'

She let out a loud gasp. 'You should've thought of that years ago. You should've thought of that before you left. Hell's Bells, Roggero! You broke my heart. I'm not sure I'll ever be happy again.'

He stepped closer.

Severine stepped back, holding her hands up in front of her.

'No! Don't you dare. Don't look at me like that. I mean it, Roggero. Don't come near me. Don't you even think about it!'

'It seems I can think of very little else, Severine. I am as surprised by this as you are.'

'What? What are you saying? Are you actually telling me that you still want me? Is that what you're saying? After all these years?'

He took another step closer. She took another step back.

Her eyes were wide, her lips were parted, her expression betrayed the turmoil in her mind.

'It seems I do.'

He stepped even closer. She did not move.

'And … and you honestly expect me to believe that?' She gave a derisive laugh but it caught in her throat and sounded more like a whimper. 'Come on, Roggero. I'm not the stupid young woman I once was. You can't seduce me with your words like you did back then. With those sultry looks. I'm not going to simply fall back into your arms, if that's what you think.'

'You were never stupid, Severine. And from memory, I believe you seduced me as much as I seduced you. With your words. Your sensual looks. I do not expect you to fall into my arms but I am hoping that perhaps, we might fall into each other's.'

'I … I'm engaged.'

'I know.'

'I'm pregnant.'

'I know.'

She stared at him; her eyes filled with doubt, disbelief and something else. Something he had seen so many times before.

'The last time I told you I was pregnant, you vanished into thin air.'

'I know. And I am truly sorry.'

'And it was your child then. This time it's not.'

'I am well aware of that, Severine.'

He reached out and brushed a lock of hair from her face.

'Don't touch me,' she said. But her voice was soft and she didn't move away.

'I cannot help it.'

'Is this because you saw me kiss Logan last night? Are you thinking that I'm easy? That because I kissed some other guy, I might be prepared to kiss you too? To do more than kiss you? Is that what you're hoping?'

'I think you wanted me to see that kiss. But I do not think you are easy. You are far from easy, Severine. I believe you are the most difficult woman I have ever known.'

'I didn't mean easy in that sense. I meant easy as in—'

'I know what you meant. You are not easy in either sense. And I do want to kiss you. But not because I saw you kiss another man. I have wanted to kiss you since the moment I saw you again after so many years and so much heartache.'

'Heartache? What do you know about heartache?'

'More than you can imagine.'

'Really? You ran away and left me, Roggero.'

'I know. But I am here now. And believe me when I say this, Severine. I am not going anywhere. I will never run away again.'

He grabbed her hand and pulled her to him and kissed her as if he didn't want to let her go.

Because that was exactly how he felt.

And he wanted her to know that.

He needed her to know that.

No matter what happened next.

Chapter Thirty

Severine heard a sort of strangled shriek and the thud, thud, thud of shoes against the floor as she and Roggero finally eased themselves apart. From the corner of her eye, she caught a glimpse of Evie disappearing along the hall.

Oh Hell's Bells. Had Evie seen them kissing?

'I think Evie saw us,' Roggero said. 'We should talk to her.'

'And say what, exactly?' She met his eyes but quickly looked away. 'I'll talk to her, Roggero. And I need some time to think about what just happened.'

'Are you unsure?' He placed his hands on her shoulders.

'Unsure of what? Of how I feel? Of us? Of this? You bet your life I am. I need to speak to Evie.'

His hands slid down her arms and as she turned away, his fingers caught hers.

'Severine?'

'Please, Roggero. Let me go and speak to my sister. Let me think.'

He nodded and in an old-fashioned gesture, drew her hand up to his lips and kissed her fingers.

'Take as long as you need. As I have said, Severine. I am not going anywhere.'

He smiled at her and she smiled back before hurrying after Evie.

She found her sister sitting on a window seat at the end of the long hallway, staring out into the twilight.

'Evie. Can we talk?'

Evie didn't turn around. 'It's finally stopped raining. The clouds are slowly dissipating and it looks as if it's going to be another beautiful night. That huge moon is already casting silvery strands through the gaps in the clouds. Yes. We can talk, Severine. And perhaps you can tell me who else you're planning to kiss.'

'That's not entirely fair, Evie. I didn't plan to kiss Roggero. It just happened.'

Now Evie did turn around, but she remained seated.

'It just happened?' Evie nodded. 'And last night? With Logan. That just happened too. I'd better make sure I don't leave you and Zachary alone. It might just happen that you'll end up kissing him.'

'Evie! I wouldn't. You know I wouldn't.'

'Honestly? I'm not sure about that. What are you doing, Severine? I know you said you thought you might still have feelings for Roggero, and I know you said you used to have a crush on Logan, but dear God. You can't just go around kissing every Tom, Dick and Harry. You really need to get a grip. You need to sit down and decide what – and who – it is you want, because if this carries on, your name will be mud. You may not care, but I think your daughter might. And Mum and Dad certainly will. And Gran. And me for that matter.'

Severine shook her head and flopped down beside Evie.

'I know. I know. I'm trying, believe me.'

'Try harder.'

'It's complicated.'

'You can say that again.'

'I don't know what to do.'

'Stop kissing people, for a start.'

Severine smirked. 'That's easy for you to say. I can't seem to help myself.'

'Try Sellotape. Or glue. Stick your lips together and keep your mouth firmly shut. And stay away from attractive men. In fact, stay away from all men, just in case.'

'Join a nunnery?'

'As quickly as possible. Or go and live on an island.'

'Snowflake Isle is an island.'

'A deserted island. With one palm tree for shade.'

'If only I could find one.'

'I expect Zachary will know where one is. In fact, I expect his grandfather owns one. And he's got a private jet.'

'Joshua Thorn? I expect he does. He seems to own rather a lot of things from what Gran said.'

'Ah. Gran told you the 'Joshua' story, did she?'

Severine nodded. 'Did you know Grandad was so hopeless with money? We might've been rich if only he'd known what he was doing.'

'Being rich wouldn't help you now. Except that Gran might own an island. And a private jet. But being rich wouldn't stop you kissing people, left right and centre.'

'No. Possibly not.' Severine laughed. 'But I'd be wearing diamonds when I kissed them. And I wouldn't have money worries.'

Evie nudged her. 'Do you have money worries?'

Severine shrugged. 'I always worry about money. I think it's in my genes.'

'But … are you in debt, or anything?'

'Not really. Maybe a little bit. Don't look at me like that. Honestly, I'm fine. It's just a few thousand pounds, that's all. And Harvey is going to give me an allowance once we're married. A huge allowance. So I'll clear the credit card straight away.'

'An allowance? Good God, Severine! What a horrible picture that conjures up. Please tell me that's not why you're marrying him. Please say it's not for money.'

'It's not. Honestly. But you've got to admit that marrying a rich man isn't exactly a disaster.'

'It's a total disaster if the money's more appealing than the man. Go and tell Gran right now. She'll give you the money to clear your debt. You know she will. And she'll give you money to live on if you're struggling. And if things are really that bad, you can always come home to live.'

'To Snowflake Inn?' Severine shook her head. 'Can you really see me living here again?'

Evie nodded. 'Yes, Severine. I can. But if you can't bear the thought of living with all of us in this inn, I expect Gran would help you rent something nearby. She might even help you buy somewhere of your own. And Raven loves it here. She's far happier here than she is in London. And far happier than she will ever be in New York, I suspect.'

Severine sighed. 'I want Raven to be happy. But I do love Harvey. Honestly I do. It's not just because he's rich.'

'So you keep saying. And yet, you've only been back a day or two and you've already kissed Logan and Roggero. Go and talk to Gran. Clear your debt. Get some cash in the bank. And then decide how you feel. You might start seeing things in a whole new light.'

Shafts of silver moonlight crept through the window and unfurled in front of them, stretching out along the length of the hall.

Severine and Evie exchanged glances.

'A whole new light. Like … the moonlight?' Severine said, grinning.

Evie nodded and slipped her arm through Severine's. 'Yep. And if you make the wrong decision, we'll blame it on the moonlight, and start all over again.'

Chapter Thirty-One

'It's stopped raining,' Luna said, smiling at her uncle. 'If it's OK with you, I'd like to go out and take some photos. The moon is incredible again tonight.'

'Of course it's OK with me. You know you don't have to ask for my approval or permission. This is your home now for as long as you want it to be. You can come and go as you please.'

'Thanks, Mason.' Luna kissed him on the cheek. 'Do you need anything before I go? I'll be back in a couple of hours.'

Mason shook his head. 'I have everything I need right here.' He tapped the table beside him, where Luna had earlier placed a glass, a decanter of port and a plate of cheese and biscuits next to his book. 'You take as long as you want. Pop back into Michaelmas Bay if you like and go for a drink with Chris. As I said, I don't know him that well, but I'm sure he'll get you home safely tonight. Or tomorrow, if you prefer. You did seem rather taken with him, from what you told me.' He chuckled and winked.

'Mason!' Luna laughed. 'I simply said he was nice and that he made me laugh and feel at ease. I didn't say I wanted to jump into bed with the man.'

'Well. If you decide you do, just send me a text so that I know where you are.'

'If I do decide to go into Michaelmas Bay – and I'm not saying I will, although it would be good to get some photos of the boats and the Bay with the moon on the water – but if I do, I'll still be home by midnight.'

'Have fun.'

Luna blew him another kiss and left.

'Where are you off to?' It was Juniper's voice.

'Hi. Just going to take some photos.'

'Of the moon?' Juniper's boyfriend, Darren asked, wrapping his arm around Juniper.

Luna nodded and smiled. 'It is my speciality.'

'Yes. I saw your pictures last night. They're fabulous. We're thinking of getting one for our new kitchen, so let us know when you have some for sale. I know the ones in the restaurant are just for display purposes.'

'They belong to Mason. If you're serious, I can show you my portfolio at some stage. I've got a lot of stuff on its way from Spain, but all my artwork is saved on my laptop, so just say the word.'

'Fancy joining us in Snowflake Inn?' Darren asked. 'We can chat about it over a drink.'

'Thanks. Another time? The moon's almost full and I really want to get some shots before it clouds over again.'

'Sure. Anytime,' Juniper said. 'We're in there most nights. God. That makes us sound like bar-flys. We're not, honestly, but all our friends are there so …' She shrugged. 'Anyway. You know where to find us. Good luck with the photos. Can't wait to see them.'

They said their goodbyes and Luna set up her camera by the edge of the channel separating the mainland from Snowflake Isle. She watched Juniper and Darren as they crossed the ancient wooden bridge, now a silvery-brown as moonlight washed over it. They stopped halfway across and stood, arm-in-arm gazing down into the sparkling water below.

It was the perfect picture and Luna took several shots, making sure to get not just the moon, the bridge and Juniper and Darren in the centre, but also the beams of silver-white, splayed out across the grass, the cobbles and the water.

They would buy one of the photos she had taken, she was sure of that. And if they wanted, she could adjust the filters, the colours and any part of the image with her photo enhancing software. She wouldn't do that for everyone, but she would do it for a friend. And she already thought of Juniper and Darren as friends.

Pleased with those shots, she turned her lens towards the inn and took several shots of that. Then of the cottages behind her, and the hills beyond. She spent a very happy and satisfying hour clicking away, surrounded by the sounds of the waves bubbling against the inlets of Snowflake Isle, and the occasional squawk of a gull overhead. It was a still night and not as cold, which surprised her, but she was wrapped up against the elements, just in case.

She was enjoying herself and wasn't ready to go home. The last bus into Michaelmas Bay had long since left but it wasn't far to walk and it was such a beautiful night. She packed away her tripod and hung her camera strap over her shoulder. There would be more photo opportunities on the way.

Perhaps she would pop in to one of the pubs in town and soak up some local atmosphere. She had no problem doing things on her own. She was independent and she liked her own company. Sitting in a pub alone didn't bother her. Even if it did sometimes seem to bother other people. But after meeting Chris this afternoon she didn't fancy sitting in a pub watching other people having fun.

Maybe she should have accepted Chris' offer this afternoon in the café. He had asked her if she'd like to join him for a drink tonight. She had been tempted, very tempted, but something held her back. Instead, she had taken his number and told him that she'd call. He had asked for hers and she had smiled.

'I'm not one of those women who likes to sit and wait for her phone to ring,' she told him. 'I'll call you instead.'

'So I have to sit and wait for mine to ring? Is that fair?'

'Suck it up, mister,' she teased. 'Women have been doing it for years. It's your turn now.'

'That's OK. I can take it. I'm cool.' He pulled out his phone and checked the screen. 'You haven't called yet. Not that I'm panicking or anything. I know you'll call. You said you would. You will, won't you?' He pulled a face.

She laughed and so did he.

'I'll call. I promise.'

'I hope so. This was fun. I like you, Luna Blake. And I'll never curse the rain again. Unless you don't call me. In which case, I'll swear and scream and shout and never go out in the rain until the day I die. But you'll call. So it'll be fine.' He grinned. 'And now you're wondering where I've hidden my axe, aren't you? Don't worry. I'm not crazy. But I think, in a very short space of time, I could be crazy about you.'

He looked into her eyes, as rain bounced off the cobbles outside, and the smell of cake fresh from the oven and coffee bubbling in a pot, wafted around them and he leant forward and kissed her softly on the lips.

It took her completely by surprise – and sent a thrill to parts of her that hadn't been thrilled for quite a while.

'Yes,' he said, leaning back in his chair, his gaze still firmly fixed on her and a rather sexy smile fixed on his lips. 'I could definitely be crazy about you.'

And she could probably be crazy about him.

If she hadn't already been half in love with someone else.

Chapter Thirty-Two

Logan held open the door to the staff toilet whilst Lucy, one of his waitresses, rushed in. And she only just made it. Logan had seen projectile vomiting in his time, but Lucy's display was something he would not forget in a hurry. Today was clearly not his day. It had been one thing after another, and to top things off, he had not seen or heard from Severine.

'I'll leave you to it, Lucy,' he said, as gently as he could. 'But I strongly suggest you go home and go to bed.'

'No. I'll be …'

She clearly wasn't fine – assuming that was what she was going to say before the force of nature intervened. He let the door swing shut and got her a glass of water, returning moments later and softly tapping on the door.

'May I come in?'

He took the grunt as a yes and quietly pushed the door open. She turned her ashen face to look at him and he handed her the glass.

'Please go home, Lucy.' He watched her drink a few mouthfuls.

She shook her head very slowly. 'But the restaurant is fully booked tonight.'

'Let me worry about the restaurant. You go home, or I'll be worrying about you too. No. I don't want to hear any argument. I'm calling your dad to come and get you.'

'OK,' she said, and quickly turned her head and vomited again.

He let the door go, pulled his phone from his trouser pocket and called her parents to tell them she was sick.

'That'll be the effects of last night,' her dad said, in a vaguely amused fashion.

'I didn't see Lucy drink much,' Logan replied.

'Not at your party, no. But she went clubbing afterwards and heaven alone knows what time she got home this morning.'

'She looks pretty grim. She shouldn't have come to work.'

'She didn't want to let you down. Perhaps she'll learn a lesson from this, but I wouldn't count on it. We were all her age once.'

'Tell her not to come back until she's better.'

'Thanks, Logan. Will you be able to cope tonight without her?'

'Yeah. It'll be fine. See you when you come to pick her up.'

'I'm on my way.'

Logan rang off and shoved his phone back in his pocket. Now he was a waitress down and the restaurant was fully booked. He didn't have any back-up staff, which was pretty dumb, considering, and he didn't know anyone who could help. He could hardly phone Severine and ask her to step in. Evie would, but Snowflake Inn was packed and even though the inn now had a full complement of staff, he couldn't expect Evie to drop everything and come running to his aid. Juniper might, but she could talk the hind leg off a donkey and would probably get all the orders wrong, even with the most up-to-date technology the restaurant was using. He didn't have a choice. He'd have to call his mum. Before he had the chance, a resounding crash of pans made his heart race and he dashed to the kitchen to see what drama was occurring now.

Thankfully, it was nothing serious. The pans were empty and were soon picked up, washed and put back on their shelves. They weren't dirty and the floor was spotless but standards had to be maintained. No sooner had that been done than the high-tech and hugely expensive coffee machine on the bar started leaking water on to the floor. Luckily for him, his sous-chef knew how to fix it and another disaster was averted with only fifteen minutes or so to spare until the restaurant was due to open for the evening. At least all the tables were set and everything was ready. He was just about to call his mum when someone tapped on the door.

'Luna!' he said, despite the fact she couldn't hear him. He put the phone down, hurried to the door and unlocked it. 'Hello, Luna. This is a lovely surprise.'

'Hi. Um. Do you need me?'

'Sorry?' He didn't understand the question and she didn't look too pleased to be asking it. She was looking everywhere but at him. 'Do I what?'

'Need me. I just saw Lucy, one of your waitresses from last night, and it's obvious she's going home.'

'Er. Yes, she's sick.'

'I gathered that much from the fact she just threw up over some man's car. So, do you need help?'

'Oh dear. That was her dad's. He won't be pleased. Um. Yes, I need help. I was about to call my mum.'

She gave him an odd look. 'Is your mum a waitress?'

'No.'

'Well I am.'

'You're an artist.'

'I'm also a waitress. Or at least I was. I worked at a Tapas Bar in our village.'

'Seriously?'

'Yes. So do you want me or not?'

'Oh God, yes, I want you! You cannot begin to imagine how much I want you.'

He saw the expression on her face and the flush of her cheeks, and heard the burst of laughter coming from a couple of the staff behind him. Only then did he realise what he'd said – and just how loudly he'd said it.

'Do you have a spare uniform? I look a bit rough.'

He looked her up and down. She looked sensational to him, but he had to agree that walking boots, jeans, and a thick jumper, just visible beneath her weatherproof jacket, were not what he wanted his waitresses to wear.

'I honestly don't know. I'll have a look in my office. I think there may be some spare uniforms in there. Sorry. Come in. And thanks so much for this. You may very well have saved my life. And I'll pay you, obviously.'

'I don't want your money. This is a one-off favour.'

'Oh. OK. Well then, you must come and have dinner one night. My treat.'

'We'll see. The uniform?'

'Yes. The uniform. Sorry. I'm not thinking straight. Follow me.'

He led her to his office and thanked his lucky stars that there were a couple of skirts and blouses hanging up in plastic covers. He remembered now that his mum had ordered extra, just in case.

'That should fit,' Luna said, pointing to the blouse he was holding. 'And this skirt.' She took it from the rail. 'It might be a bit big. But a belt will do the trick. Where can I get changed?'

'In here.'

'Then would you mind leaving me for a few minutes, please?'

'Sorry. Of course. I'll be downstairs. Thanks again, Luna. This means a lot.'

'I'm happy to help.'

He stopped at the door and turned. 'Um. I know this is none of my business, but I thought you didn't know anyone here before yesterday? Other than Mason, of course.'

She frowned. 'I didn't.'

'Oh. I could've sworn I saw you today. With Chris Lyons. From the bookshop. Holding hands. And kissing.' He closed his eyes for a nano-second. Shit. Why had he said that? And in such a robotic fashion. He hadn't meant to mention it. What was wrong with him lately?

She gasped. 'You saw the kiss?'

He nodded. 'I saw the kiss.'

'Oh.' She looked at the floor.

'Did you meet him last night? That was pretty quick work.' He hadn't meant it to sound sarcastic, but he knew it had.

Her head shot up and she glared at him. 'At least he's not engaged. And neither of us is pregnant.'

She looked horrified.

He was astonished.

'Oh God!' Luna said, clearly distressed. 'I'm sorry. I didn't mean to say that.'

He studied her face for a moment before shrugging his shoulders. 'That's OK. I shouldn't have mentioned you and Chris. Your love life is none of my business.'

'And yours is none of mine.'

He nodded and forced a smile. 'Friends?'

She nodded and her smile looked as fake as his. 'Friends.'

'Right then. I'll go before I say anything else I will regret. Come down whenever you're ready.'

He closed the door before she could respond, and kicked a pile of boxes in the hall, in frustration. But they weren't empty, as he had thought. A lava-like flow of demerara sugar erupted from the hole he had made in the side of one of the boxes, and trickled on to the floor from a couple of bags that his shoe had obviously burst.

Today was definitely *not* his day.

Chapter Thirty-Three

Severine went down for breakfast feeling like death warmed over. She had hardly slept a wink all night and had had the strangest dream. She had dreamt that she and Raven were living in a cottage. A cottage in a tiny village but she couldn't quite see where. And then she had woken up and the dream had ended. Just when she had finally dozed off again, Evie burst in, telling her that Jessie wanted everyone downstairs because she had an announcement to make.

'Can't it wait till later? I think I'm suffering from delayed jet lag.'

'No, you're not.' Evie pulled off the duvet. 'You've got five minutes to get your backside out of bed and get down to the kitchen. It's seven o'clock and the staff will be here in thirty minutes to serve the guests their breakfasts.'

'Seven!' Severine grabbed the duvet and yanked it back over her, curling herself into a ball.

'I'm not getting up at seven in the morning. I had enough early starts at work. Gran can make her big announcement once the breakfast service is done.'

'She wants to do it now. And I think you may want to hear what she has to say because she told me to tell you that it would be to your advantage.'

Severine poked her head out and glanced at Evie. 'She's just saying that to get me downstairs at this ungodly hour.'

Evie smiled. 'I think she's telling the truth.'

'Did you say anything to her about my money issues?'

Evie shook her head. 'Nope. Now get out of bed or I'll get a wet towel and drop it on you.'

Reluctantly, Severine got up and a few minutes later, followed Evie to the kitchen.

Besides Evie, her dad and her mum were there, and Raven and Jessie. There was no sign of either Zachary or Roggero but she was too tired to ask where they were. She sat at the table and Molly kissed her on the head, placing a mug of coffee before her.

'Toast, darling?' Molly asked, smiling cheerfully.

Severine shook her head. 'Just coffee. Thanks for this.' She raised her mug and drank half its contents without stopping to take a breath, then stretched her arm out on the table and rested her head on it.

'Now we're all present and correct,' Jessie said, throwing Severine a sidelong glance. 'I have something I want to say. I don't want any interruptions and I won't be repeating it so listen carefully – and that means you, Severine.'

'I'm listening!'

'Then sit up straight and stop slouching across the table.'

'Hell's Bells. Give me strength.' Severine sighed and sat up but flopped back against the chair as soon as Jessie looked away.

'John, you are my only son and you know I love you with all my heart, but you're almost as bad with money as your dear father was.'

'That's not very nice,' said Molly, somewhat indignantly.

'But it's true,' John said, with an affable smile.

Molly shrugged and Jessie continued:

'As I was saying. Now that I have all this money, I felt I should make plans for the future. Joshua has arranged things so that I won't pay any taxes while I live. Don't ask me how but there it is. All his money is offshore. Before, I would have called it devious. Now I'll call it a wise investment decision and good money management.'

'Is that legal?' Raven asked.

'Apparently, it is,' Jessie replied. 'Anyway, he tells me I can give each of you a small, tax free sum as a gift and I'm doing that today. Ah. I see I finally have your attention, Severine. Don't get too excited. The tax free allowances aren't large. But I believe in staying within the law. I've made a will, and you'll each get an equal share of everything when I die, but I'm planning to stay around for many more years yet. I simply wanted you all to know that this money is as much yours as it is mine and my dear, departed William's.'

Everyone said, 'Thank you,' in unison, and Jessie smiled.

'And there's something else. And I want everyone to hear this. Severine, I don't know what your plans are for the future, and I'm not convinced you have any idea yourself, but I know your family, including me, would like you here more often. This inn is busy now, thanks in no small part to Zachary and his show. Raven has a room here. So does Evie. Zachary has one room booked on a permanent basis for himself. Roggero is here, although he's going to move to Michaelmas Bay shortly, I understand. You should have a room here too, Severine, but the way this is going, the inn will be half full of members of this family and their loved ones – or former loved ones. So I've decided that it's a good idea for me to invest in some other property, both in Michaelmas Bay and in Snowflake Cove.'

'What other property is there in Snowflake Cove?' Evie asked.

'The Beadleshaws are putting their cottage on the market. They want a quick sale and I've told them I will buy it. We're instructing solicitors this morning.'

'The Beadleshaws?' Evie said. 'I didn't know they were thinking of moving.'

Molly nodded. 'It's true. They told us yesterday evening in the bar. What with everything else going on yesterday, I completely forgot to mention it last night before we all went up to bed.'

'So,' Jessie said. 'If you like, I'll rent their cottage to you and Raven, Severine for, what Joshua tells me is called, a peppercorn rent. But you can keep the peppercorn. I don't need an answer right now. I'm buying the cottage in any event. But the offer is there. I just wanted you to know that.'

Molly clapped her hands together as if in silent prayer and beamed at Jessie and Severine. 'How wonderful, darling! Isn't that perfect?'

Raven bounced up and down on her chair. 'Say yes, Mum. Please say yes!'

Severine's mouth hung open until Jessie's words sunk in and she looked at Evie. 'You said you didn't say anything to Gran.'

Evie shook her head and smiled. 'This is all her idea. I haven't said a word. I didn't even know about the Beadleshaws.'

'I don't know what to say, Gran.' Severine reached out and squeezed Jessie's hand. 'That is very generous. Really generous. But I wasn't planning on staying in Snowflake Cove, I don't think.'

'You'll only be renting,' Jessie said. 'You're giving up your rented home in London anyway. If things don't work out with Harvey, you'll need a place to stay and it's getting far too crowded here.

Besides, it needn't be permanent. Unless you decide you'd like it to be. You could come and go as you please.'

'But …' Severine looked at Raven's excited face, and smiled. 'Then, yes. I'd like that very much. Thank you, Gran. This means a lot to me. And to Raven.'

Molly jumped out of her seat and hugged Jessie first, then Severine, so tightly that Severine could hardly breathe. Raven hugged Severine then Jessie. Evie did the same, and finally, Severine's dad hugged everyone.

'This means the world to all of us,' John said.

'And Evie.' Jessie took Evie's hand in hers. 'I'll do the same for you if you like. Although we may have to wait a while for another cottage in Snowflake Cove and I know you're perfectly happy living here. And with Zachary around, I don't think you'll be needing help from me in any case.'

Evie hugged Jessie again and smiled at Severine. 'I can always move in with Severine.' She winked. 'That was a joke, Severine. I'm very happy where I am.'

'You are very welcome to move in with me and Raven, anytime.'

Severine looked around at her family and their happy faces and smiled.

Was this really happening? Had she really said yes? Had she actually agreed to stay in Snowflake Cove, even for a little while?

Raven was jumping up and down again. 'We're gonna be living in Snowflake Cove.'

Reality dawned on Severine like a wet shower. But it was a warm, wet shower. Not bad, exactly. Just rather surprising. And she was suddenly wide awake.

She and Raven would soon be moving into a cottage in Snowflake Cove. Albeit on a temporary basis. She couldn't move here permanently. And she'd have to give Harvey some sort of explanation for her prolonged stay.

But this would give her time to think. Time to really decide where – and with whom – she wanted to spend her life. It would give her and Raven a home of their own.

It was like a dream come true.

Her dream. The dream she had last night.

Hell's Bells!

How bizarre was that?

It was almost as if this was meant to be.

As if it was what she really wanted. Or at least what her subconscious wanted.

Chapter Thirty-Four

Luna awoke to the smell of coffee; she jumped out of bed and rushed downstairs. Mason was in the kitchen making breakfast and he beamed at her when she entered, rubbing her eyes.

'Good morning, sweetheart. Look! I believe there's been a marked improvement.'

He had both feet on the floor and was only leaning on one crutch.

Luna gave him a joyful smile. 'That's wonderful, Mason. But please don't overdo it. Here. Sit down and let me finish making breakfast.'

He hesitated for a moment but soon gave in and sat.

'Tell me about last night,' he said, his eagerness to hear about it, evident from his tone. 'Did you get some great photos? Did you have fun? I believe I heard you come home around midnight. Thank you for the text to let me know.

That was most kind of you to go to Logan's aid. I hope he showed his appreciation. But of course he did. He's such a kind and thoughtful young man.'

'I did get some great shots,' Luna said, putting the toast Mason had started, on to a plate and handing it to him. 'The restaurant was packed, and yes, Logan was grateful. He kept thanking me on the way home in his mum's car. She came to pick us up because she wouldn't let Logan drive yesterday.' She smiled at the memory of that.

'Mum's coming to get us,' Logan had said, as they were closing up. 'She insisted I couldn't drive and she was probably right to do so. I got so drunk at my opening party that I couldn't remember a thing. Not even kissing Severine.' He gave her an odd look but she ignored it. 'Not one thing. Except for looking at the moon – and you.'

'Me?' She almost dropped the bag containing her clothes she'd changed out of earlier.

He nodded. 'You.'

She hurried to the door. 'Well. Um. It was a beautiful moon.' She needed to quickly change the subject from the night of the party. 'And it's just as gorgeous tonight. I took lots of photos before I got here. I was hoping to take some more on the way home but it's clouded over now.'

He closed and locked the door behind her. 'Oh shit. Have I ruined your night? I'm so sorry. But I'll make it up to you.'

'You haven't ruined anything.' She kept a safe distance between them as they waited for his mum.

'The forecast for tomorrow is good so I'll get more shots tomorrow night. You don't need to make anything up to me.'

'I want to. Especially as you won't let me pay you for tonight.' He moved a little closer.

She moved further away.

'Will you need me tomorrow, do you think? Lucy did look rough. Let me know if she calls in sick and I'll come and give you a hand.'

'What about your photos?'

'I'll take some on the way here and some on the way home.'

'I can't ask you to do that.'

'I offered. It's no problem. Call me. I've texted you my number.'

'You're really kind, Luna.' He took a step towards her. 'I don't know how I would've coped without you here tonight. So I'll make you a deal. Whether Lucy comes to work tomorrow or not, when I close up here, I'll take you up to Michaelmas Great Wood. There's a spectacular view from there, and you'll get some very artistic shots of the moonlight through the trees.'

'It's a date,' she said, as one tiny strand of moonlight filtered through the clouds.

He smiled at her in a way that made her tremble – in a good way. A very good way.

'It's definitely a date.' He moved closer. 'I'm looking forward to it already. And Luna. About last night, I …' Bright light hit them both full on, and it wasn't from the moon. 'Bugger. It's Mum.'

And once again, something magical between them had been broken.

'Are you helping out again tonight?' Mason asked, spreading marmalade on his toast.

'What? Oh yes. Possibly. Logan's going to call me. But he's offered to take me out after he finishes work, to get some photos in the woods.'

'In the woods? How delightful. Michaelmas Great Wood is a magical place, even in daylight. At night, beneath a full moon, it'll be a breathtaking sight.'

It wasn't the only thing that would be a breathtaking sight.

It would have competition from Logan Dorset's smile.

And how would Luna cope with that, alone with Logan in the woods, beneath the moonlight?

Chapter Thirty-Five

Severine had some thinking to do. Jessie's offer was beyond generous as well as a complete surprise. But the most surprising thing to Severine was the fact that ever since breakfast she had become more and more excited about the thought of living in Water's Edge, Winnie and Arthur Beadleshaw's cottage.

In London, she and Raven shared their home with a friend. To have a home of their own had always been one of Severine dreams, but a dream too far out of reach for her to achieve alone – until now.

A home for her and Raven was one of the things that Harvey could provide. But Raven had made it clear that she didn't want what Harvey was offering them. And Severine must put Raven first.

Of course there was now the new baby to also think about. This was Harvey's child as much as it was Severine's and the reality of that would take some working out. Could she marry Harvey and persuade him to spend their lives flitting back and forth between New York and Snowflake Cove? Was that even feasible? It would certainly be exhausting. And would it be fair to either of them?

She had finally spoken briefly to Harvey yesterday after making excuses and sending texts, and had told him that she may need to delay her return.

'Whatever you need, honey,' he had said, clearly not bothered either way.

'Just a couple of weeks or so. Raven may be difficult to persuade.'

'Want me to come over?'

'No,' she said, a little too quickly. 'I think it's best if I sort this out alone. I'm just not sure how long it may take.'

'That's fine with me, honey. It'll take whatever it takes. You get some rest. And don't you go overdoing things, you hear?'

'I hear. Speak soon then.'

'OK, honey. Love you.'

'Love you too,' she said.

But now she wasn't quite so certain that she did. At least not as much as she should.

But she had some breathing space. Time to think things through. And now, with Jessie's offer, she would have a home to do that in.

The air was crisp and cold today, but the cloudless sky was blue. It was March now and would soon be spring. Crocuses and snowdrops popped their heads out of the grass on the cliffs of Snowflake Isle, as if someone had scattered brightly coloured beads as far as the eye could see. The first few leaves of the daffodils were forcing their way out to find the sun and Severine smiled as she crossed the bridge to the mainland. Water's Edge cottage was just on the other side and her chest swelled as she imagined living there.

'Hello Severine!'

'Logan! I didn't see you there.' He was walking towards the bridge from the direction of Jane's cottage. 'Where are you off to? Oh, the restaurant I suppose.'

He nodded, pointing towards the car park opposite. 'Just getting the van. How are you? I haven't seen you since … my party.'

'Ah yes,' she said, covering the distance between them. 'I think we need to talk about that night.'

'Yes, Severine. I think we do.'

'Could we talk in your van? It's cold out here and I don't think Jane, or your mum, would welcome me in for coffee. And I'd rather not go to the inn.'

'Are they giving you a hard time?' He smiled compassionately.

'Actually, no. They're not. But I think this conversation should be private. Don't you?'

'I suppose that's best.'

They walked in silence to the van, which only took a couple of seconds. He held the door open while she got in, before climbing in beside her and swivelling on the seat to look her in the eye.

She met his look and took a deep breath.

'I'm not sure why I kissed you, Logan. It was possibly a mistake.'

'Well. Let's not beat about the bush. That's pretty to the point.' He smiled wanly. 'Do you regret it, Severine?'

She shook her head. 'No. I suppose I should, but I don't.'

'I don't regret it either. And I don't regret telling you I loved you. I've wanted to do that for years.'

'Logan I … I don't know what I'm doing.'

'That makes two of us. I've loved you all my life, Severine. I put you on a pedestal.'

His voice was calm and almost matter-of-fact. His eyes were clear and bright. There wasn't a hint of the passion and longing she had seen that night, and he kept his hands to himself.

'I know. I like you Logan. I like you very much. But I'm not sure I could love you. Not in the way you deserve to be loved. And I'm not sure that you would really want me to.'

He shook his head slowly. 'I thought I did. I thought I wanted to hear you say those words more than I wanted anything in the world. Even yesterday, I thought that. Until last night.'

'Oh?' She smiled at him. 'What happened last night?'

'Lucy, one of my waitresses, threw up.' He grinned at her and ran a hand through his hair.

'Delightful! And that made you realise that you didn't love me anymore?' She laughed. 'I think I should be offended. But I'm not.'

He laughed too. 'It wasn't Lucy being sick. It was Luna standing in for her.'

'Luna? Oh. Mason's niece. I met her on the train.'

'I know you did. I met her shortly after.' His brows furrowed, but the smile quickly returned. 'Something happened when I saw her, but I didn't realise what at the time. Then at the party I was going to kiss her. But you stepped in.'

Severine shook her head and hit herself on her temple with her hand. 'Trust me! I'm so sorry, Logan. You should've told me to get lost.'

He grinned. 'I was too drunk to know what was happening. But when you kissed me, I forgot about Luna because all I could think about was that all my dreams were coming true.'

'Nightmares, I think you mean.'

'No, Severine. Dreams. Something I had wished for all my life. But the thing is, we should be careful what we wish for.'

'Because when we get it, we realise it's not what we want. I know that feeling, Logan.'

He nodded. 'I do still love you, Severine. But it's an idealistic love. A long-held fantasy. The reality can't possibly live up to that. Being Luna last night at the restaurant finally made me realise, it was the thought of you I loved. I realised I didn't want to spend my life with you. Grow old with you. Have a family with you.'

'But you do want to do that with Luna?'

He shook his head. 'I've only just met her. I think it's too early to say. And yet … when I look at her … Well, it's like they say in the movies. I feel as if I've come home. Does that make sense?'

'Complete sense. I just hope she feels the same about you.'

'Shit, Severine, so do I.' He laughed. 'I can't have another lifelong infatuation with a woman who doesn't feel anything for me. The problem is, I think she may already be seeing someone else. I'm taking her to Michaelmas Great Wood tonight. I'm hoping I'll have my answer then.'

'You're taking her to a wood? On a date?' She sighed, and swivelled in her seat, placing her hands on Logan's shoulders. 'I think I know where you've been going wrong as far as women are concerned. Let me give you some advice.'

'Advice on love? From you? Are you sure?'

They looked each other in the eyes and burst out laughing.

Chapter Thirty-Six

Severine got out of Logan's van and made her way back across the bridge to Snowflake Inn. It was as if a great weight had been lifted from her shoulders and she felt happier than she had done for a long time. Her heart to heart with Logan had done this. Perhaps it was time to have a heart to heart with the other men in her life. She had already told Harvey she was staying put for a while. And the truth of the matter was that Harvey had not seemed at all concerned. Perhaps he would understand if she told him she was having doubts about their future. They would still have their child to consider and the logistics of that might not be easy, but she was sure they could work that all out. But first, she needed to talk to someone else. And she needed to be honest with herself.

She had been in love with Roggero Tazzeone for most of her adult life. She had dreamt of sharing her life with him. Dreamt of bringing up

Raven together. But he had disappeared without a word and broken her heart in two, in the process. Since then, the truth was, she had compared all men to him. And all men, until Harvey, had come up short.

Perhaps she couldn't teach Logan anything about love, but perhaps Logan could teach her. Had she put Roggero on some sort of pedestal? Had she idolised the fantasy instead of the reality of him?

If the things he had said to her since she had come home, were true, it seemed there was a possibility that she might be able to have what she had secretly wished for, for most of her life. If she got it, would she want it?

She still loved Roggero. She was sure of that. But did she love him enough?

What was it that Jessie had said? Before you can love someone else – truly love someone else – you have to love yourself.

Had Severine ever loved herself?

Yes, she had been selfish. Yes, she expected everyone to run around after her. Yes, she always wanted – and frequently got – her own way. But that wasn't loving herself.

Loving herself meant she would be confident. She wouldn't need a man to give her the things she wanted for herself and for her children. She would be happy facing a future without a man to support her... if she really loved herself. And she certainly wouldn't settle for a man simply because he could solve her money worries. Now, thanks to Jessie, she had no money worries. She would have a home for herself and for her children.

On a branch of one of the trees nearby, she heard a bird singing sweetly, and as she walked, she smiled.

Finally, after all these years, she knew exactly what she wanted. It was as if the light had dawned. She also knew precisely *who* she wanted.

She wanted to find herself. To be – what had Raven said? Nicer. She wanted to be the best person she could be.

Out of Harvey and Roggero, she knew, if she had to, she would choose Roggero. But the truth was, she didn't have to choose. She could have both men in her life – as friends. And maybe, in time, she would have one of them as her partner. Or perhaps she would meet someone else. It didn't matter. What mattered was that she loved them both. She wanted them to be happy. But it was time she learnt to love herself. To be happy with her life. To spend time with her family and her own children. In their own home. Roggero would be welcome. So would Harvey. But neither would be moving in.

The future was something she could think about much later.

Her present was looking very bright and she was going to enjoy it.

Chapter Thirty-Seven

Luna was nervous. In spite of telling herself all day, every hour, on the hour, that she had no reason to be; because tonight was not a date with Logan, in the romantic sense. It made no difference. She paced the floor; sat down and got straight up again; went out and came back in; picked up a book and put it down. She couldn't concentrate on anything. More than once, Mason had asked her what was wrong. Each time she had replied that there was nothing wrong. What could be wrong?

At precisely eleven o' clock, Jane had come for coffee, so she said. The truth was, she had come to tell them the news. And what glorious news it was. Although at first, Luna had thought it was all bad.

'Have you heard the news?' Jane asked, obviously knowing full well they hadn't. 'Jessie is buying Water's Edge. Winnie and Arthur are moving. I have to say, they kept that quiet. I had no idea. But apparently neither had anyone else until last night. But you'll never guess who will be moving in. You won't, so I'll tell you. Severine!'

Luna had nearly dropped an entire cup of coffee over Jane's lap but thankfully managed to steady her hand in time.

'Severine is staying in Snowflake Cove?' She hoped her voice didn't sound as horrified as she felt.

Jane nodded frantically. 'Yes. Yes. Can you believe it? I know it's true because I've just been at the inn for coffee with Jessie and she told me herself.'

Mason smiled devilishly. 'I'm surprised you're happy with this news. I thought you couldn't wait to see the back of Severine.'

Jane gave him a look of reprimand. 'I admit it's no secret that I don't like Severine very much. The woman has no morals. And I have to say, I'm not convinced she'll change. But apparently, she says she wants to try. I only caught the gist of it because I happened to hear a conversation she was having with her sister. This was before I had coffee with Jessie. But Jessie said she didn't know the ins and outs, just the result.'

'And that is …?' Mason asked.

'Oh. Well, Jessie told me about the cottage, but I overheard Severine tell Evie that she had come to a decision. She is going to stay here and bring up both her children. Both, mind you. And that she is going to break off her engagement. Can you believe that?'

Luna swallowed the lump in her throat. 'Why?'

Jane looked her in the eye. 'Because she has decided she doesn't love him enough to marry him. And that's not all. She is going to tell Roggero that for now, she only wants to be friends with him. I'm not sure what that means. I wasn't aware he had asked her to be anything else. But you know those two as well as I, and I'm sure it won't be long before they're carrying on with one another again.'

'And Logan?' Luna held her own cup steady.

'Logan? Oh. You heard about that nonsense at the party. Well that's all over and done with.'

'Is he … upset?'

'Of course he isn't. I knew it was all just a silly mistake and that he would soon come to his senses. He's a good boy. A lovely young man. He deserves someone far better than Severine Starr. And strictly between the three of us, I think he has his eye on someone else. He told his mother and me that he'll be very late home tonight. And there was something in his manner that indicated it had nothing to do with work.'

Jane winked and Luna choked.

'Are you quite well, my dear?' Jane asked. 'You seem to be all of a flutter this morning. I hear you helped out at the restaurant last night. That was very kind of you.'

233

She glanced from Luna to Mason and back again and there was something in her eyes that told Luna that Jane Dorset was putting two and two together and making a new romance.

'That's the doorbell.' Luna leapt from her chair, never more thankful to be saved by a bell.

'Luna Blake?' someone asked from behind a huge display of flowers in which two long ribbons held two large helium balloons. One in the shape of a crescent moon and the other, a full moon, both with faces painted on them

'Yes. I'm Luna. Are these for me?'

'That's what it says here.' A woman about Luna's age, tipped her head sideways around the blooms, and beamed at her. 'Someone likes you, Luna Blake. Someone likes you a lot.'

That seemed a very odd thing for a florist to say.

'Thank you,' Luna said, taking the flowers from her.

'And I think we both know who that someone is.' The florist winked. 'Logan wrote the card himself.' She waved goodbye, and was gone before Luna could say another word.

'Was that Lisa?' Jane asked from the doorway of the sitting room. 'Oh, good heavens! What beautiful flowers. Are they for you? Who are they from? Did I hear her mention Logan's name?'

'Um. I believe so.'

'What does the card say?'

'I haven't read it yet.'

'Well come along.' Jane disappeared back into the sitting room, obviously expecting Luna to follow.

Before she did, she read the card. It said:

'Thank you for last night. I'm hoping tonight will be even better. Until then, I'm sending you some moonlight. Logan. xx'

Not exactly romantic. And yet …

'We are waiting,' Jane called out.

So am I, Luna was tempted to reply.

Chapter Thirty-Eight

Logan felt as if his entire future hinged on what he said and did tonight.

Lucy had called to say she had recovered and would come to work, so he called Luna to tell her he would pick her up once the restaurant was closed.

'No. I'll come to you,' she said. 'I can take some pictures on the way. And thank you for the flowers. They are beautiful. And the balloons.'

'I'm glad you like them. If you're coming here, why not come for dinner?'

'You're fully booked. I saw the bookings last night.'

'I can find you a table, Luna.'

'Thanks. But I'll eat with Mason. He wants to go to Snowflake Inn tonight. I said I'd go with him if you didn't need me to work.'

'That's a coincidence. Mum and Gran are going there tonight. Gran wants to find out all the gossip.'

'I know. She told us. I think that's why Mason wants to go, too.'

'To find out gossip? Or to be with Gran? Don't worry. I know he's got a crush on her. And between you and me. She is keener on him than she makes out.'

'I can tell.'

'Can you? I'm usually hopeless at such things.'

'Are you?' Luna sounded as if she doubted that.

'Yes. Unless someone actually tells me.'

'What? Tells you they've got a crush on you?'

'Yes. And even then, I'm pretty hopeless.'

'You didn't look … Sorry. I have to go.'

What had Luna been about to say?

'I'll see you tonight, Luna.'

'Yes,' she said. And she had hung up without saying goodbye.

Chapter Thirty-Nine

'You called!'

Chris sounded happy, which made Luna cringe. She hadn't wanted to make this call. She had to though. It was only fair. He seemed so nice and she didn't want to string him along, whether or not something happened tonight between her and Logan.

'Hi,' she said. 'I'm afraid this isn't good news.'

'Oh. Don't tell me. You've met someone else.'

'I had already met him. I should've told you before we went for coffee. I'm sorry. He hasn't even asked me out. But the thing is, Chris. I want him to. And that's not fair on you.'

'So this is one of those, it's not you, it's me, type of calls?' He laughed. 'Don't worry. I'm joking. Crap comedian, remember?'

'Lovely man, with a lovely smile, is what I remember.'

'Not the kiss?' He laughed again.

'It was a lovely kiss.'

'Thank you. I enjoyed it. You've got my number, Luna. Call me if it doesn't work out. I'll try and think of some better jokes. Good luck in love.'

'Good luck to you too, Chris.'

Chapter Forty

Logan had never seen the moon so bright, or seemingly, so close to earth. It looked as if it would collide with our planet at any second, knocking us, like a billiard ball, way off into a distant galaxy. Or more likely, knowing his luck of late, into a black hole.

Well, wasn't that a cheery thought?

All evening, he had been on edge and when Luna tapped on the door a little before midnight, he almost jumped out of his skin.

'Hi,' he said, opening the door for her. 'Would you like a drink? Or something to eat? How are you? You look lovely. Have you taken many photos? It's a beautiful night. I kept peering out the window at the moon. Sorry. For some reason, I seem to be rambling.'

Luna smiled. 'Hi. It's certainly a beautiful night, and I'm fine, thanks. Are you ready?'

'Ready? Oh, yes. I'm ready.'

He locked the door and they walked side by side to his van.

'Any gossip?' He opened the door and held it until she was seated.

'Lots,' she said, when he got in and sat beside her. 'I don't know where to begin.'

'Anywhere you like.'

He started the van and drove towards Michaelmas Great Wood.

'Severine is staying in Snowflake Cove.'

He glanced at her. There was something in the way she said that which made him a little uneasy.

'I know. She told me.'

'Oh? When did she tell you?'

'This morning. I met her on my way to the car park. We had a chat.'

'A chat?' There was a catch in Luna's voice.

'Yes.'

'Did she … Did she say anything else?'

'Yes. She offered to give me some advice on my love life.'

'Your love life?'

He darted a look at Luna. 'Yes.'

She quickly looked away and fiddled with the button of her jacket. 'Do you need advice?'

He laughed. 'Severine seems to think so. And I think she's probably right.'

'Really. What sort of advice?'

'About why it's wrong to take someone to Michaelmas Great Wood on a date.'

He shot another look at her and saw the startled expression on her face.

'I … I don't understand. Was she saying it was wrong for you to go on a date?'

He smiled. 'Nor did I. And no. That wasn't what she was saying. She was saying my choice of venue was a mistake. I thought it was a great idea. Which is probably why I need advice.'

'You don't need advice. It is a great idea. I mean … that is … Is this a date? Are we on a date? Or are we just looking at the moon?'

'Can't we look at the moon and be on a date at the same time?'

'Yes, of course. I meant …'

He reached out and took her hand in one of his, keeping the other firmly on the wheel.

'I know what you meant, Luna. Yes, this is a date. And I'm hoping it's the first of many.'

'You are?' She sounded like a church mouse.

'I am.'

'So am I,' she said, looking at him from beneath her lashes. 'But what about Severine? I … I thought you loved her.'

He pulled up at the entrance to the wood and, letting go of her hand, engaged the handbrake.

'I thought so too. And I did. But not as much as I thought. We're just friends.'

'Are you sure?'

'Absolutely.'

He got out and opened the passenger door, took her hand again and led her to the back doors of the van.

'Ta dah!'

He threw them open and Luna looked inside, before beaming up at him.

'A picnic? You did all this?'

'I wasn't sure how long we'd be and I thought it might be cold.'

He had spread a blanket on the floor of the van, piled several cushions around the edges and filled a wicker picnic basket with, he hoped, delicious treats from his restaurant, a bottle of champagne, and glasses. He had also bought some time controlled, battery-lit candles which he had placed here and there around the sides.

'It's a wonderful surprise. Thank you so much, Logan.'

He was the one who was surprised when she stood on tiptoe and kissed him. It was just a quick kiss. No more than a peck on his lips but he thought that someone, somewhere must be letting off fireworks.

'That was a wonderful surprise,' he said, smiling down at her.

He reached out and took her in his arms. 'I really like you, Luna. I like you a lot.'

'And Severine?'

He frowned. 'Do I like Severine?'

She shrugged. 'Are you really over her?'

'Absolutely. I'll be completely honest. I never thought I would be. But what I felt for Severine wasn't real. It started off as a crush, and when Dad died, and we stopped going to Snowflake Cove for our holidays, the thought of Severine became an obsession. I made her into someone who wasn't real. I promise you. I'm over her. And you?'

'Me?' She laughed. 'I was never in love with Severine.'

He grinned at her. 'You know that wasn't what I meant. What about Chris? Are you going to be seeing him again?'

She shook her head. 'No. I'd already fallen for someone else.'

He moved slightly away from her. 'Someone else?'

'For you, Logan. I'd already fallen for you.'

'You had?' He held her tight again. 'I wasn't sure. On the night of my party when we stood outside and looked at the moon, I thought perhaps you had. I know I was falling for you. But then … Severine came and … I don't quite know what happened. Personally, I blame it on an age-old crush – and too much to drink.'

'And this? What do you blame this on? The way we feel for one another. Shall we blame this on the moonlight?'

He shook his head slowly and smiled. 'No, Luna Blake. You can blame it on the moonlight if you like, but this, I think, may well be love at first sight.'

Then he kissed her to show her exactly what he meant, and from the way she kissed him back, she wasn't blaming it on the moonlight either.

She agreed with him.

What they felt for each other was love. Or at least the very start of love.

And nothing could be blamed for that.

Especially not the moonlight.

THE END

Coming soon

See my website for details.

A Note from Emily

Thank you for reading this book. A little piece of my heart goes into all of my books and when I send them on their way, I really hope they bring a smile to someone's face. If this book made you smile, or gave you a few pleasant hours of relaxation, I'd love it if you would tell your friends.

I'd be really happy if you have a minute or two to post a review. Just a line will do, and a kind review makes such a difference to my day – to any author's day. Huge thanks to those of you who do so, and for your lovely comments and support on social media. Thank you.

A writer's life can be lonely at times. Sharing a virtual cup of coffee or a glass of wine, or exchanging a few friendly words on Facebook, Twitter or Instagram is so much fun.

You might like to join my Readers' Club by signing up for my newsletter. It's absolutely free, your email address is safe and won't be shared and I won't bombard you, I promise. You can enter competitions and enjoy some giveaways. In addition to that, there's my author page on Facebook and there's also a new Facebook group. You can chat with me and with other fans and get access to my book news, snippets from my daily life, early extracts from my books and lots more besides. Details are on the 'For You' page of my website. You'll find all my contact links in the Contact section following this.

I'm working on my next book right now. Let's see where my characters take us this time. Hope to chat with you soon.

To see details of my other books, please go to the books page on my website, or scan the QR code below to see all my books on Amazon.

Contact

If you want to be the first to hear Emily's news, find out about book releases, enter competitions and gain automatic entry into her Readers' Club, go to: https://www.emilyharvale.com and subscribe to her newsletter via the 'Sign me up' box. If you love Emily's books and want to chat with her and other fans, ask to join the exclusive Emily Harvale's Readers' Club Facebook group.

Or come and say 'Hello' on Facebook, Twitter and Instagram.

Contact Emily via social media:
www.twitter.com/emilyharvale
www.facebook.com/emilyharvalewriter
www.facebook.com/emilyharvale
www.instagram.com/emilyharvale

Or by email via the website:
www.emilyharvale.com

Printed in Poland
by Amazon Fulfillment
Poland Sp. z o.o., Wrocław